Edited by Aquila Editing

Cover Designer: Bookin It Designs

HER DEVIL NEXT DOOR

A MAY DECEMBER ROMANCE

ABBY KNOX

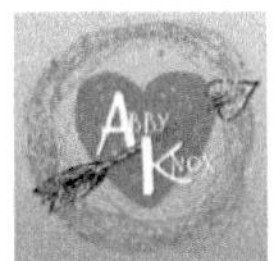

HER DEVIL NEXT DOOR

Colette

On the outside, I'm just another suburban girl from an upstanding family. But behind closed doors, my life is sheltered and controlled. At age 22, I should be having fun and sowing my wild oats. But socially, I'm so far behind everyone else my age, it's embarrassing. I need a change. When a mysterious older man moves in next door, I seize the chance to learn more about the world outside of my father's tight control. What begins as innocent flirting soon turns my entire life upside down.

Warrick

I moved to this neighborhood to retire in peace and quiet. But the family next door gets my hackles up. There's something strange about them. Specifically, their daughter seems far too interested in me and my desire for a dull, suburban life. The more I push her away, the more I'm drawn to her. Colette's wide-eyed innocence unsettles me, and her thirst for knowledge ensnares me at every turn. When I discover what's really going on next door, I have no choice but to take extreme action that could upheave the anonymous solitude I've fought so hard for.

This wide-age-gap, girl-next-door romance contains no cheating, no cliffhangers and is a stand-alone story with a happily ever after!

ONE

Colette

I NEED to stretch my legs.

Logging off my final online class for the day and perusing my day planner, I make sure I've ticked all the boxes before taking my free time. Sewing? Done. Calligraphy? Completed. Baking? Just uploaded a photo of my latest project, and the pie is chilling in the fridge.

I should be free to absorb some much-needed Vitamin D. Ha. Not that kind of Vitamin D, unfortunately. Not while I'm living under my parents' roof. They are super strict about visitors, and even though I'm 22, I've never even been on a date with a guy.

No, the only D I consume is the kind that's plentiful in the Sunshine State. But I don't mind so much. The weather in Florida may be more humid than the inside of Satan's jockstrap, but I'll take any chance I can to escape the house and soak in the sun.

The sound of an approaching car prompts me to lift my

gaze to the picture window. Peeking up from my studies, I see the postal carrier's truck park at our street-side mailbox. I jump from my chair. "The mail's here! I'll get it!"

My father looks up from his studies on the far side of the library.

"Have you finished school?" He still speaks to me like I'm 15 and not a full-grown woman.

"Yes. I'm wearing my latest project, see?" I twirl. He eyes my outfit, and I see his lips twist. I know that look. I hold my breath and wait for the criticism. As for me, I like the flowing fabric in this heat, especially since my parents are so stingy with the air conditioner.

"That skirt is too short, and your shirt is too tight. Change, and then you can go."

I lower my head. "Yes, sir."

He doesn't like my sullen tone, but lately, I'm tired of his rules. But if they shut me out, then where would I go?

I finger the lace on the edge of my skirt, finding myself silently wondering if drawing attention to my body is that much of a bad thing.

"Immodestly provokes impure thoughts in men. Is that what you want?"

I don't answer.

Mom scolds him. "Oh, Jarvis. It's just to the mailbox and back. Let her go."

Dad shoots a reproachful glance at Mom and then looks back at me. "Fine. Go. But make it quick."

I bound out the door like a puppy newly freed from her crate. The sun and the ocean breeze wafting over the golf course feel good on my skin. I spend most days in my room, library, or the living room doing online school, so I take a chance to go outside whenever I can.

"School" is a bit of a stretch. I graduated from my

private high school at 16. My parents have me taking online lessons to teach me "how to be a good wife," they say. Cooking, baking, sewing, knitting, crochet, and cross stitch are just a few classes I take. They've also enrolled me in various online study groups, religious book clubs, etc. Paper-making was my choice. I love all forms of art, and I sneak it in under the guise of wifely duties. I convinced Dad that when the time came for me to marry a suitable man, I could impress him with my frugality by creating homemade wedding invitations. That clinched it. Old Jarvis Roberts will buy into just about anything if I sell it as a reflection of my good upbringing.

His primary motivation for keeping such a leash on me is because he's the pastor of our church and everything we do is a reflection on him.

Once outside, I admire my mother's vining clematis that winds around the quaint brick-covered mailbox at the end of our long driveway.

From our mailbox, I can see the ninth hole; the vivid green of the trees and gentle hills tempt me to take a stroll. I never learned how to golf, but I might like to learn.

I inhale the scent wafting from the row of red rose bushes that separate our driveway from the newly built two-story next door, and I hear the zippy sound of Candace Walker's golf cart approaching.

The hunter green cart squeaks to a halt, and Candace calls to me when I reach the end of the drive. "Hey, babe! When are you coming to work with me at the golf course?" Candace and I went to high school together, and she's the closest thing I could call a real-life friend. Most other kids our age went to college and then never came back. It's comforting to see her whenever I go outside the house.

Candace turned 21 a few weeks ago and has been

working almost every shift that the Rosewood Glen Country Club will give her and earning mega tips. She rarely has time to walk with me in the mornings anymore, but I'm happy for her; she seems to be having a blast in her new job.

I eye Candace's adorable pink short-shorts, golf shirt, and visor—her cocktail server uniform. I imagine wheeling around all day in the sunshine on that lovely golf course, tanning, and making my own money.

I applied for a job at the golf course, and the course manager said he wanted to hire me on the spot. My dad shut it down. "Serving alcohol is unladylike," he'd said. I'm not sure what that means because half of the people I've ever seen serving and drinking alcohol are women.

"Soon, I think!" I lie to Candace, as upbeat as possible. I can't bear how some people look at me. Other women in some of my virtual classes, like my friend Lily, tell me to grow a spine and stand up to my dad. But they don't get it. I don't know anything different.

"Great!" Candace replies, "'Cause this summer is gonna be huge, and we need you. These old farts tip well, and there's a fresh wave of new members with all the new houses going up. Gotta run!"

We wave goodbye as she zooms up the street and heads to the club around the bend.

Candace will graduate from community college next year, and after that, she's not sure. She might travel. I'm not going to lie; I'm envious.

I've looked online at the art programs at some state schools, and they look like an absolute paradise. What I would give to be in a room with an instructor, models, and other like-minded people. Mom and Dad would never speak to me again if I stepped out of line and applied to a school they didn't approve of. And there's a lot they don't approve of.

But sometimes, I do step out of line.

Having a little secret keeps me happy. It gives me something to look forward to. Mom and Dad get stressed out over the church finances — and fielding phone calls from the members — so they sometimes take sleeping pills. Whenever they do, I sneak back downstairs to fetch my laptop and take it to my room.

Sometimes I stay up all night, learning everything I've ever wanted to know about sex. I've seen ... things. Let's just say it's a good thing I clear my history after every use. I know they check it.

Reaching into the mailbox and pulling out the electric bill, Mom's gardening magazine, and Dad's monthly haul of religious tracts, I'm reminded of how weird our life must seem to everyone else. Do they know what really goes on? Do they know that my dad and his parishioners drive to the city every Saturday to hand out pamphlets about fire and brimstone and the end being nigh?

What is "nigh," anyway? What's with the Old English? Are they just trying to sound spooky? Honest to God, the end has been "nigh" for so long you'd think they'd have come up with a different talking point. But the Rev. Jarvis Roberts loves an energetic apocalypse sermon.

As I stand there staring at this armload of mail, a car's approach catches my attention. A sleek, silver Mercedes glides past me, so close that I startle out of my thoughts.

The darkened windows reveal a faint silhouette of a broad-chested man with a beard. The car pauses, and the driver exits.

I am thunderstruck at the sight of him: A perfectly tailored suit in a color of blue that I can't identify. It's not navy, nor is it midnight. It's set off by a silk, textured neck-tie, and crisp white shirt. As he stands, his veined, strong hands fasten the top button of his suit jacket. My eyes travel upward, along the line of a broad shoulder, taking in the full salt-and-pepper beard that's more pepper than salt. His thick eyebrows bear a few stray silver strands, as does his thick, close-cropped hair. His face is imposing and severe, with a strong nose that reminds me of my brief class in Renaissance art. My dad pulled me out of that class when he noticed my fascination with the statue of Michelangelo's David. ("They should cover their privates as God intended.")

This stranger's large brown eyes bear crow's feet, but I'd guess not from smiling. No, his smiles are hard-won. Slight sun damage dapples the parts of his face I can see. And then I wonder, how he can stand maintaining such a thick beard in this heat?

He looks me straight in the eye, all business. "After-noon." He nods, his voice flat but not unfriendly.

I open my mouth to speak, but air comes out. My throat is dry despite the humidity. "H-hi. Are you the new neighbor?"

I glance away from his gaze to the "Sold" sign stabbed into the lawn next door.

A pause brings me back to his eyes, which travel down to my neck, and I watch his Adam's apple bob before he answers. Another curt nod. "Warrick Jameson. And you are?"

Warrick. The name sounds medieval. I picture him swinging a broadsword, lobbing off heads on the battlefield.

"Colette. Colette Roberts." My name makes me self-conscious, and I feel myself blushing. It sounds so prim and goody-goody. That's precisely what I am, though.

He repeats it back to me. "Colette."

Warrick doesn't say, "Nice to meet you, Colette," or "May I borrow a cup of sugar, Colette?" Just my name.

In his mouth, my meek mouse of a name sounds new. His gravelly voice and thick lips wrap around it, sending my name back to my ears with the ferocity of a stolen kiss.

His dark beard twitches slightly. "Colette," he says again, this time with a hitch in his throat as if he needs to clear it. As if he's trying to hold back some emotion. On Warrick's sensuous lips, "Colette" sounds like sin wrapped in worship.

The way he's looking at me while he says it, it's too much.

I say his name back to him because it seems like the thing to do. "Warrick," I say, then swallow the ache in my throat.

Warrick's nostrils flare. The consonants dominate my lips, forcing my mouth into a shy smile at the end. It feels like a curse word. Sometimes at night, when I'm frustrated with my father's rules, I yell the word "fuck!" into my pillow, and I find the "k" sound to be therapeutic. Lily says "fuck" a lot when we chat online, making me laugh. The thought of that filthy word, and that his name reminds me of it, makes me smile a bit bigger.

To the casual observer, this is just two neighbors making awkward introductions. His eyes flick to my mouth for half a second. It's barely detectable, but I see it. I could stand here and melt in the heat as long as I was allowed to stare at that face a little bit longer. That imposing, masculine face. My hands itch to draw those eyes, crow's feet, lips, and furrowed brow. My fingers can feel that soft beard as I visualize positioning Warrick's face to capture the perfect light. He would be an excellent subject; he has the aura of a predator who could sit still and wait for hours while I draw him. Wait, and then pounce. Take what he wants. Warrick oozes stamina, patience, and a dark, specific type of hunger.

I wonder what he sees when he looks at me and says my name like that. In his eyes, I must be a strange, pale little bird.

Another presence looms behind me. I have to go. I break our shared gaze and glance up at the house, where my father stands in the picture window of the library.

What is he doing, gaping at us like that?

"Nice to meet you, Warrick. Welcome to the neighborhood." I offer him a smile that barely disguises the foreshocks of the coming earthquake in my body. My sex has never trembled this forcefully in response to anything or anyone, not online or in person.

The physical presence of this man, his eyes, the cut of his jacket, his choice of necktie...even the hairs on the back of his hand, and that deep voice—all of it has teased out something powerful from this good girl.

I know what this is: Pure lust. A misplaced desire, unfortunately, because Warrick is older than me. Much, much older. Twenty years at a minimum. Holy moly. The differences between us are almost breathtaking.

Warrick has to be older than Dad. I shouldn't be yearning to touch a man that age. That's...that's wrong, isn't it?

Confused and alarmed, I turn tail and sprint to the front door, hearing my name repeated in my head in Warrick's deep voice. "Colette. Colette."

I feel like I might pass out from the heat, and all I crave is a glass of water. Sweat drips from every pore of my body. A wave of desire slicks my panties. The muscles there contract against nothing, and I find myself wishing to be rid of these wet clothes. All of them.

I can't get indoors fast enough.

When I'm finally dousing my parched throat with ice water, I realize my one mistake. I dropped Dad's parcel of religious tracts in the driveway.

TWO

Warrick

POOR COLETTE, I frightened her.

She'd flown to her front door, dropping a thick envelope on the pavement and leaving the mailbox wide open.

Colette must have the impression that I bite. My lip twitches with an uncontrollable smirk.

No, Warrick. You're fifty-two. She can't be twenty-five yet. And she's your neighbor. Way to ruin the block party when you just got here.

And yet, I entertain specific thoughts. It's harmless if it's all in my head, right?

Taking her for myself would be so easy. She's ripe. Curious. Her gray, searching eyes told me everything. She longs for company, for someone to talk to her. Her soft, parted lips, with questions ready to spill out. She's like a startled, adorable kitten who doesn't yet know the power she wields over humans with her sweetness. I could say the word and have that sweet thing in my bed the next second.

I could show her just how mighty she is.

Colette looks timid, but her soul crackles with thunder. Imagine how voracious she would be; imagine what I could teach her.

You just moved here. What would they say at the club?

Yet I can't deny what's between us. Her friendly facade betrayed her authentic self when I held her gaze. The mood that had passed over her face in the few seconds of conversation spoke of such loneliness. Hopelessness. Thirst.

First, she smiled at me. And my heart broke open. Then, her face darkened when she realized that man was watching us through the window. Her husband, perhaps? Doubtful. Married women approach me far too often; Colette doesn't possess the easy flirtatiousness of a woman who's someone else's wife.

Colette's lips slowly wrap around my name, making me imagine so many depraved things she could be doing with that mouth. And now, I'm standing here, knocking on her door.

The man who stood in the window a moment ago now fills the open door in front of me. He has Colette's face shape and an overall family resemblance, but none of her brightness or curiosity. Yet he looks too old to be an older brother. Behind him, a woman with eyes like Colette's stands up. She wears a housecoat and clutches a gardening magazine.

There are no lights on, except for a dim reading lamp by a wingback chair. This room has no bright Floridian decor or style one would expect; the place feels like a movie set funeral home from forty years ago. Dark wood, heavy brocade curtains, plush wall-to-wall carpet, and fake flowers. It's all designed to convey wealth, but it is fussy and dated.

The energy in here gives me the creeps. And that's coming from a 52-year-old man who just got turned on by his new twenty-something neighbor. Something strange is going on in this house. What exactly it is, I don't know. By the posture of these people, I can guess that this man rules with an iron fist. And that's just the beginning.

"Colette forgot this." I hold out the thick manila envelope, and the man takes it from me.

With his other hand, he reaches out to shake mine. "I see my daughter has already been bothering you. Jarvis Roberts."

Her father. I'm flooded with math problems. The man has to be younger than me by ten years. And if his daughter is still living with him, that means she's not even as old as I thought she was. Oh god. I'm a fucking monster.

I nod and introduce myself. "Not a bother at all; Colette's a lovely girl."

Ignoring the man's slight bristle at being corrected about his daughter, I look past his shoulder and offer a smile and a nod to the woman in the housecoat. "You must be Colette's mother."

She smiles. "Grace," she says. "Welcome to the neighborhood."

Colette appears, then, carrying a water bottle. Her hair has been hastily tied in a top knot, and stray, damp tendrils cling to her neck. "Does anyone want some lemona—"

Her body freezes stiff at the sight of me at her door.

Wolf and kitten have spotted each other, both of us ready to pounce.

This isn't right. *Go away,* I try to tell her with my eyes.

"You must come for dinner tonight. Please, let us welcome you to the neighborhood properly," Jarvis suggests.

I shake my head and smile. "I wouldn't want to impose.

But thank you, maybe another time." My delivery is polite but clipped in hopes that Jarvis will take a hint.

Colette's shoulders fall; her frame seems to shrink into itself. I've disappointed her by refusing dinner.

On Grace's pushback, I quickly relent. "It's no trouble; we'd love to have you if you have no plans. Besides, it's just the three of us, and we have a huge roast beef."

Although everything about this place unsettles me, I muster every ounce of charm and manners my mother taught me. "That sounds awfully tempting."

Colette's brows turn upward in a hopeful expression. The aroma of a roast and potatoes wafts in from the kitchen, further tempting me. I haven't eaten since after my run this morning.

Grace claps her hands together. "You'll dine with us? How wonderful."

What century is this lady from? Why are these two so strange, and Colette seems so...different?

I grimace. "You talked me into it."

Jarvis and his wife confirm the time of dinner with me, but I'm not listening. I'm only devoted to reading the body language of the young, alluring Colette. A shy smile passes from her to me.

She's pleased. Too pleased.

It's just dinner, Warrick. A supervised dinner. Get through it, and never associate with these bizarre people again.

Colette may be a sweet young woman, but exploring these feelings any further will lead to trouble.

THREE

Colette

I SIT CROSS-LEGGED among the pillows of my bedroom's window seat—my favorite reading nook—and I write his name in my daily devotional journal with a deep blue ink pen. *Warrick.*

It's silly, but my mind has latched on to his name and the color of that suit. The veins in his hand as it fastened the button while he looked into my soul.

A warm rush floods my body.

I need to know the name of that color blue of his suit.

I set my journal aside and pick up my laptop, looking up all the rich blues I can find on the Pantone website.

My mind wanders as I click, click, click. The blue of his suit is just a shade darker than his eyes. His beard enchants me even more. So thick and just the other side of needing a trim. A hint of wildness at the edges, like a virile, decadent King David. I've read the Bible forwards and backward, and nobody can tell me that character didn't have a mile-long hedonistic streak.

What must it feel like for a beard to brush up against one's neck? Would it tickle? Would it hurt?

Heat prickles over my skin at the thought. I close my laptop because I can't think straight. Looking out the window, I stare at the light bricks next door, the color of Cream of Wheat.

The hairs on the back of my neck stand up suddenly. I'm being watched. My gaze goes straight to the window directly across from mine.

Warrick.

I cover my mouth in surprise when I gasp. He looks as if he'd been in the act of removing his suit jacket and happened to look over. I must have startled him as much as he surprised me.

Yet he doesn't look away. Neither do I.

As a silent need cries out below my midsection, I uncover my mouth and let my hand drift to my tummy.

Seemingly in response, Warrick lets his suit jacket drop from his shoulder. Slowly, he hangs it on a wooden hanger and smooths out the fabric as if for my benefit.

Why does watching him care for his clothes stir my body's deep, dark places?

I want him to caress me that way. I've not been hugged by anyone since Candace hugged me at my high school graduation when I'd graduated two years earlier.

Is this wrong? The two of us standing here, watching each other out our respective bedroom windows? I mentally scan the house. Mom and Dad's room is downstairs in the opposite corner of the house. The only other room with a window facing Warrick's home is the library, adjacent to the living room. We're safe, I tell myself.

Safe from what, though? Safe from being caught doing what?

I don't know how much time has passed, but my salivating mouth dries up when Warrick finally makes a move. He steps closer to the window. And then, his hands—those veiny, strong hands—unbutton his shirt.

He's dressing for dinner. That's all he's doing. But is it? *He's looking right at you. He's undressing for you, you poor, silly dear.*

I should stop this. Close the curtains and run away.

I don't do any of that. Instead, I watch his hands. I have to because the eye contact might just kill me.

Recovering from the shock of what's happening here, I drag my hand up to my sternum as if bracing for my heart to pound its way out of my chest. With the way my pulse races, this is a distinct possibility.

One by one, the buttons loosen, revealing his white tank underneath. His dress shirt falls away to reveal tanned, broad shoulders and a beefy chest. Just enough hair to tempt me. I don't know what I would touch first if I had the chance. His beard? Or his chest? Or would I have a choice? Would he call the shots?

My mouth drools. Should I change my panties before dinner? No. Why ruin two pairs in one day?

Tearing my eyes away from his chest, our gazes lock on each other. Predator and prey.

Never in my life has a boy paid this much attention to me. But I'm not interested in boys. Or any other men. Warrick's piercing blue eyes are the only ones I care about.

And then Warrick does something unforgivable. Stretching out his arms, his hands rest against the window frame. The movement makes the solid muscle of his shoulders bunch and ripple. This pose broadens his chest further, showing off the hardness in his bare arms. Those thick traps and triceps. The veins on the undersides of his forearms are the worst cruelty. My mind is full of filth now. All I can think about is running my tongue over all that sinew, his rough edges.

I want to do things I've seen in some of the videos I've watched in the middle of the night when I sneak my laptop upstairs. I want to pin him to the mattress and ride that beard until we break the bed.

I can't help but lick my lips.

Something happens to Warrick's face then. His expression changes from patient predator to hungry warrior. It's then that I realize my hand has wandered away from my sternum to one hardened nipple.

Idle hands are the devil's playthings.

But indeed, touching my own breast by accident will not send me to hell. Not if I confess right now. That's what I'll do. I'll confess, then go to dinner and not feel tempted.

Abruptly, I stand up and close the curtain, pick up my devotional book, and sit on my bed. I must confess my sinful thoughts this instant, then go and set the table.

I draw in a breath, fold my hands to pray, then look back at the drawn curtains at my window.

And I think. And think some more.

I've entertained this thought before...how can something that feels good and right be wrong?

As if they have their own mind, my hands pull away from each other, finger by finger.

I skip my confession and go downstairs to set the table with a smile on my face.

Warrick's coming to eat.

FOUR

Warrick

I'M NEVER GOING to make it through this dinner.

Jarvis and Grace are going to know. They'll be able to tell I'm guilty of something. I've corrupted their daughter.

As Grace smiles and passes me the roast potatoes, I nod and glance at Colette. The latter sits directly across from me at this round mahogany dining room table. Her chest is flushed pink, at least the part that I can see in the vee of her shirt.

I clear my throat and concentrate on passing the potatoes to Jarvis. *Eat your dinner, make polite conversation, and get out of here.*

"So, what do you do, Jarvis? Grace?"

Grace chuckles dryly and smooths down a lock of hair that doesn't need smoothing. "Oh me? I'm just a housewife."

I smile at her. "Nothing 'just' about it. I'm sure you're the glue holding this family together."

She blushes and nervously nods across the table.

"Jarvis is the pastor of our church."

I inquire blandly about the details of this church, but I don't absorb anything he says. Something under the table has caught my attention instead. Specifically, a delicate foot has come to rest on top of mine.

Good god.

Swiftly, I pull my foot away, expecting poor Colette to startle. I don't want to be rude, but she needs to know she can't play footsie with me under the table. But it's not Colette who starts. Grace hops slightly in her seat and sucks in her breath. "Oh! I mean, sorry to interrupt. I'm going to check on the pie."

I cannot believe this. First, Colette ensnares me, but it's her mother who tries to touch me. Well, I'm not interested in Grace. Besides, I'll never look at another woman again now that I've met Colette. I may not be able to have her, but she's bewitched me against considering anyone else.

"Colette," I ask, enjoying watching her eyes widen at being addressed directly. "Where do you go to high school?"

Surprised at my question, she shakes her head and laughs. "I didn't realize I look so young."

Her tinkling laugh is a balm to my dark soul, and I want to hear it again.

Jarvis answers for her. "She graduated at 16."

I haven't taken my eyes off her. I have to know. "And how old are you now?"

She bites her lip and pauses her hand, which has stabbed a piece of potato and now holds it midair. She arches an eyebrow at me ever so slightly, turning her head. She eyes me with an edge of playfulness. "I'm 22."

Not just a twenty-something. A young twenty-something who can't stop egging me on with her sweetness, beauty, and flushed skin every time I look at her. I'm coming undone.

She smiles while I squirm like a worm on a hook. Jarvis is talking on and on about something. He can keep talking. Neither Colette nor I are paying any attention.

The phone rings; I hear Grace answer it with a wary greeting. Seconds later, she comes into the living room, sounding flustered. "It's Mitch from church again."

Jarvis stutters, "I t-told you what to say, woman."

Well, this is getting uncomfortable.

"But honey, he keeps asking about ... you know."

Grumbling, Jarvis gets up and roughly takes the phone from Grace. Colette's mother smoothes her hair, says something breezy and dismissive, and then retreats into the kitchen.

Every moment of this dinner is torture.

At the start of this gathering, I thought I might not make it through the evening because I was dying of shame over my attraction to my neighbor's young daughter. Now, the tide has turned. I'm no longer ashamed but eager to drag Colette away from these people. I don't know what's going on with them, but it's clear to me Colette doesn't belong here.

I almost don't notice Jarvis returning from his phone call. He sits, snaps his linen napkin with a flourish, and places it back on his lap. "What line of work are you in, Warrick?"

Snapping away from Colette's wide, curious eyes, I reply, "I'm a consultant. I advise municipalities on how to streamline their public accessibility hierarchy structures."

Grace titters as she returns with the pie. "That's a mouthful."

I nod graciously as she sets down the pie and begins

dishing it out in little dessert plates. "Key lime pie. I hope you left room for dessert! It's extra tangy!"

Colette's eyes are trained on me so hard I can practically feel them thinking about unbuttoning my shirt.

"I certainly did, Mrs. Roberts," I say, emphasizing the Mrs. She blinks at me, but I tell her with a sidelong glance that I'm not going to mess with a married woman.

"I made it with love," Colette says, licking meringue off her fork. She doesn't even have to try to look seductive. She's just a young woman eating a slice of key lime pie, and my cock is so fucking hard it might break my zipper.

Jarvis clears his throat. Grace looks salty over her daughter getting more attention from me.

Jarvis nods and says, "A consultant. Huh."

Colette keeps the conversation going. "That sounds exciting. I bet you've traveled everywhere." God, I love watching her eat that pie. I grip the fork as my mind conjures up an image of me licking that sticky, sweet tartness off her round, pert breasts.

I nod at her, trying to keep my composure and sounding like a robot. "I have been to many different countries and all over the United States. All fifty states."

The way Colette's eyes light up when she asks me questions fills all my darkness with light.

She asks, "Have you ever been to Italy?"

"I have."

"Which part?"

"Rome, Florence, Umbria, Milan, the Amalfi coast."

Colette pushes her plate away and places both hands over her sternum, letting out a long, loud sigh. "That is my dream vacation. I love Renaissance art so much. And Roman architecture. I want to go and see everything. And draw everything!"

I fold my hands over my plate, rest my elbows on the table, and lean forward. "You're an artist," I remark.

"Colette enjoys her crafts," Jarvis says. I wish I had a human-sized flyswatter to make that man disappear.

Colette's stare falls to the table and the corners of her mouth droop.

"He means," Grace cuts in cheerfully, "we encourage her in the arts, within reason."

Rubbing the itchiest patch of my beard—a habit of mine when I choose my words carefully around twits like Jarvis—I focus on Colette.

"You must go to Italy. And Prague. And the Louvre. Every artist should travel. Go out, experience life," I say. *And I'll be the one to take you to all those places. Anywhere and everywhere you want to go, I'll be by your side, bankrolling the entire trip.*

Colette now looks sad. "Sounds like you don't stick around one place for very long."

I see what's happening. "I'm currently taking time off to write a book," I say, hoping to reassure her.

Colette's entire demeanor changes when she hears me say that. She sits up straight, eyes wide with fascination. "Are you writing a book about your life?"

The interest from this young woman touches my heart, and it breaks when I have to let her down.

"I'm afraid my life isn't all that interesting. No, I'm writing an instruction manual as a companion for my consulting business. Supplemental materials for groups that hire me. It's technical, boring stuff."

Colette smiles widely and shakes her head. "No way, I'm sure it's fascinating! I've always wanted to write a book. Good for you for taking the time for yourself to do it."

This young lady has so much spark in her; I can't wait to

see her absorb all the greatness the world offers. The Sistine Chapel. Michelangelo's David. The Mona Lisa. She deserves all of that and more. And all of it will look utterly pale next to her radiance.

"You're still young. There's still time to write a book. Perhaps after you tour the world, you'll have amazing stories to put down to paper."

A strange, bewildered silence falls over the table, save for the clinking of dessert forks.

I feel that if Jarvis and Grace have their way, Colette isn't going anywhere anytime soon.

FIVE

Colette

"THAT'S ENOUGH DESSERT, COLETTE."

Warrick's fork pauses in midair as he's about to take a second bite of the pie.

I've devoured my first slice, and I'm about to dive in for a second.

Dad doesn't like it when I overindulge. Plus, he's glowering because Warrick has been waxing about my future travels and what I deserve. And Dad doesn't like me eating up that sort of attention, either. Lily would say he's salty. I can't help but smile, thinking of my online friend.

Poor Warrick looks confused. Then, to my shock, he sets down his fork and pushes his dessert away. "You know what? I'm suddenly not feeling so well. Forgive me," he says, nodding to my mother and father. To me, he casts a brief glance. His beard twitches like he wants to say more. But he doesn't.

As he disappears out the door, I want to chase after him.

Of course, I don't. I wouldn't know what to say to him if I did do something so forward. He's turned off by my sweet tooth, so I might as well face facts. I think I might cry.

"Excuse me," I say, pushing away from the table and heading to the living room to grab my laptop.

Dad's voice calls after me. "Young lady. The dishes."

I mutter as I mount the carpeted stairs, "Clear them yourself, for once."

Upstairs in my room, my heart thumps like an angry fist. I've never sassed my father that directly before.

I close my bedroom door and let the angry tears fall down my cheeks. How could Dad humiliate me like that in front of a guest?

I wait to hear the arguments begin downstairs. My father lecturing my mother that my impudence is all because of her leniency, and my mother telling him he doesn't understand how sensitive I am. This is usually followed by my mother coming upstairs to urge me to apologize to my dad. "You just have to go along to get along until your Prince Charming arrives and you fly from the nest."

None of that comes, however.

Weird.

Instead, there's another phone call. More loud, frazzled whispers. Dad sounds put-upon at being interrupted at dinner, even though dinner's officially over now.

I open my laptop and post on the private Discord server. "I hate to be such a whiner, but my dad just embarrassed me in front of company by not letting me have a second slice of pie. Dessert is literally the only fun thing I get in this house."

Lily's not online at the moment, so I turn to the only other thing that helps me move past these moments. Plopping down on my window seat, I pick up my sketchbook and open it to a blank page. Here, at sunset, this spot has the best lighting.

Almost automatically, I find myself sketching Warrick's hand.

I may have forgotten how to pray, but God help me; I remember every vein, every knuckle crease, every hair on his hand.

When I finish, the hand I've sketched looks so realistic that I think it might reach out and touch me from the page.

"Colette."

The voice of God startles me so severely I jump out of the window seat and dump my sketchbook on the floor. Pencils and erasers fly in all directions.

My once-calmed heart rate starts to race again, and I cover my mouth in fright.

Once again, I hear it. "Colette, I can see your outline on the blind."

Breathing deeply, I raise the shade.

Of course, it's Warrick. Once again, his face is visible in his open bedroom window. This time, the glass is lifted. That explains why I could hear him. I open my window sash, letting cold air-conditioned air outside.

"You scared me to death!" I say with a laugh.

"I'm sorry for frightening you. I...wanted to see you."

Blinking at him, I ask, "Are you feeling better?"

Warrick's eyes darken, and he props himself up against the window frame like before. Only now, when he moves out of the shadow, he's shirtless.

Gods and monsters! So much skin. So many planes and ridges and...two burly man tits. I stifle a giggle. I don't want him to think I'm laughing at him. I'm laughing at myself and how delighted I am to see them. The swirls of masculine hair across that broad chest, a squeezable tummy, leading down...and down, guiding my eyes to a slightly soft belly and the vee lines below his belt.

I catch myself staring, my eyes exploring too much.

"Colette, I wasn't feeling ill."

"I know," I say after a long pause. "You left because you were disgusted by my taking a second helping of dessert. Gluttony is a deadly sin, you know."

Warrick doesn't say anything for a few moments but then scoffs angrily. "Gluttony? You can't be serious. Eat as much pie as you want; I don't give a fuck. I left because I was disgusted by the behavior of both of them."

He emphasizes the word "them," so I know he's talking about my parents and not me.

I swallow the feeling that's bubbling up. "Not...not by my sweet tooth?"

His beard twitches, and his Adam's apple bobs. His gaze is too intense, threatening to undo everything I understand about myself. "Never. You're perfect the way you are."

It's sweet to say, but he doesn't understand anything about anything. "That's not how it works. We are in a prison of our own making and cannot free ourselves from damnation without forgiveness...."

I don't know why I'm reciting these words. I haven't believed any of it—maybe ever. But these recitations clang around in my head louder and louder the more I find myself entranced by my neighbor. I am afraid of what I feel for him.

He cuts me off, his furrowed brow creasing even more deeply. "Forgiveness for what? You've done nothing wrong."

"You don't know me."

He pauses then and smiles coldly. "Oh, I'll tell you what I know."

I swallow again, casting my eyes around the room for a water bottle, but I've got nothing.

Warrick proceeds to read me. "Darling girl, you are a good, kind, innocent, naive child of a self-styled man of the cloth."

I blink but say nothing. Self-styled? What does that mean? We stare at each other for a long time.

Changing the subject because I don't want to talk about my bully of a father, I ask, "How old are you, Warrick?"

"I'm fifty-two." He puffs out his chest.

I smile. "Let me tell you something. You're older than my father. He might be a tyrant, but he takes care of us." I sound like my mother. I'm panicking and grasping at anything that will help me feel better for running away from my feelings.

He laughs. "You need more than what he can provide."

What am I doing? The more I try to think of the good things my father has done for me, the more I don't believe it. The more I say out loud, the more I realize how ridiculous my situation is.

This knowledge must show on my face.

"What are you thinking about, petal?"

The word "petal" makes me flush pink. "I...I'm thinking about how this has to be wrong. But something is happening to me that I don't understand. I've been unable to do anything but draw you from memory all evening."

He cock his head in surprise. I've said too much.

"You drew me?"

Biting my bottom lip, I nod.

"Let me see."

I shake my head.

"Please."

Trembling, I raise the sketchbook for him to view.

Warrick crosses one arm over his chest and strokes his beard with his other hand.

"You've made me look better than I actually look."

I release the breath I'm holding, having been worried that he'd criticize my technique.

"Colette," he says softly, causing my eyes to close as my body thrills at that sound. I feel his voice waft across my skin, impossibly. He can't touch me from across the grassy alleyway between our side yards, yet I felt him. He may as well be using those hands, those exquisite knuckles, to tease out my nipples. He could be whispering my name against the inside of my thigh, high up, where the skin is damp and untouched.

"You should study art, Colette. I know people who could teach you. Far away from your father. You're that good, I can tell."

He can keep talking for days on end about my education and everything he says he can do for me, but all I hear is my name. All I can feel is my dripping sex opening up like a flower, anticipating the touch from the source of that husky baritone.

"I have to go," I say, my voice trembling. The want, the need, the ache—all of it screams so loud inside my body that it's all I can do to control myself.

The bottom line is: this is wrong.

"Homework?"

If only I had that excuse. But I can't tell a lie.

"Lust," I say, "is another deadly sin."

With that, I close the window sash and walk away to get ready for bed...leaving the shade up and the bedside lamp on.

SIX

Warrick

I'M SUCH AN ASSHOLE.

If sweet Colette knew what she did to me. She'd run for the hills if she knew how goddamned rock hard my cock is under these trousers.

And I would chase after her.

Maybe I'm a dirty old man headed straight to hell. I'll happily go to hell as long as she's with me.

So it's a good thing I don't believe in any of that stuff; I just believe in her.

If she knew how badly I want to take her for the ride of her life, she might faint. Maybe injure herself, and then where would we be?

For the next few hours, I sit at my window and watch her sleep. I don't bother going to bed because I know I'll toss and turn and think of nothing but her.

Is this my life now?

At some point, I drift off to sleep. Who knows what time that was.

The following day, I wake to the sound of something plinking against my bedroom window. Instantly, without thinking, a smile cracks across my face. Heaving myself to standing, I stumble to the window and throw open the sash, leaning against the window frame.

"What are you up to?"

When Colette sees me, she warms my heart with a broad smile. "Incoming!"

On instinct, I stand back from the window at her command, and into my room sails...a paper airplane?

I pick it up, grinning, admiring the expert paper folding. I turn it over in my hand, then look back at her. She's proud of herself.

"Nice plane," I say dumbly, confused.

Colette chuckles. "Open it, silly!"

Carefully, I unfold the tight wings and nose. The square white parchment in my hand reveals a charcoal sketch of a woman. Colette. It's a self-portrait of her, wearing a simple slip that accents the curve of her hips and every soft, tempting feature. She's lying on her side on a bed, the blankets rumpled around her, where she reads a book. One slip strap has fallen from her shoulder; her hair is tied up messily. Her lips are parted, and her eyes are concentrating on the words. The slip barely covers her voluptuous breasts, her two erect nipples visible through the fabric. It might be the most innocently erotic thing I've ever seen in my life—second only to the woman herself.

I look back up at her, unsure of the words to say, but I don't have to.

"It's a self-portrait," she points out.

"I can see that. It's incredible."

Colette beams at me. "Really?"

"Really." I want to say that the sketch is so exquisite that it makes me think about touching her. Caress her face, cup one soft breast in my hand. Bathe the material of her slip with my tongue as I suck on her nipples. And of other things, like tearing apart those spaghetti straps with my teeth and exploring the heat between her legs.

Will I ever be ready to say those things to her? Will she ever be prepared to hear them?

"Colette. I'm going for a run in a few minutes...would you like to join me?"

She bites her lip. "I have class," she says.

"Skip it."

She rears back at my suggestion. "I can't do that!"

"Yes, you can," I tell her. "You're a grown-ass adult. Skip class and go for a run with me. Unless you don't want to. Whatever you want to do, it's your choice. I thought it might be easier to talk outside of our houses instead of up here like Romeo and Juliet."

She blushes and looks away shyly, both an endearing and maddening trait. On the one hand, it's adorable. On the other hand, I can't shake the feeling that there's shame involved and that it has to do with that fraud who rules over her.

This leads me to another reason to get her alone; I need to tell her what I learned about her father. None of it is complimentary.

"Romeo wasn't talking through a window. He called up to her balcony from the ground," she corrects me.

I nod. "And look how they turned out. Don't worry; I don't think our families are feuding."

Colette laughs, husky and low, further tugging at my

tenuous hold on good sense. But then, she bites one glossy lip. I wait. After a time, she looks up, smiles, and leans forward with a conspiratorial look on her face and stage-whispers, "Meet me at the walking trail by the pond in ten minutes."

SEVEN

Colette

ELATED, I don my sneakers, tee-shirt, and running shorts before I realize that Warrick, being new to the neighborhood, might not know where the walking trail is or the pond.

My mother stops me on my way back up to my room. "What are you doing?"

After reading all about my new crush, Lily asked the same question last night: "What are you doing? Thirty years older? He'd better have a big dick and a bigger bank account."

I'd replied, "He probably does, but none of that matters. He makes me feel things I've never felt before."

She'd taken a while to respond, then finally left me with: "But seriously. Be careful. You don't know what you're doing with men, and he can probably tell that. He might be grooming you."

I'd signed off angrily after that. Later on, I could see her point. But I just don't believe that about Warrick.

However, I believe he might have a giant garden hose hidden in those fine blue trousers. The thought of it makes my skin tingle.

"I said, where are you going, young lady?"

Mom and I stand on the carpeted stairs, me on my way back up to give Warrick directions to the pond, and her on her way down, clutching her devotional book in her hands. In all my flustered distraction, I'd forgotten that the family reads devotions together this morning. "I'm going for a run."

I say it nonchalantly as if it's something I do every day.

Her eyes widen, and she says out of the corner of her mouth, "The door is that way," pointing downstairs.

"I forgot one thing," I say, bolting up the stairs and nearly slamming my bedroom door. But Warrick is not in his room when I peer across the grassy alleyway. Something moves in my peripheral vision, and I look to the street. Warrick is already on his way to meet me, wearing bike shorts. I gasp. I don't know why this should shock me, but before now, I could not imagine him in shorts, let alone spandex that hugs his thighs and round buttocks. I'm weak. The pull of my body toward his is so strong I nearly fling myself out the window before I remember that I'd probably break my ankle.

Heading back downstairs, I'm out the door before my father realizes what's happening.

"Colette?" is all he says as he stands in the open doorway.

I smile and wave, then head slowly up the street, forty paces behind Warrick.

All this time and escape was that easy. I'm out the door. I'm free.

As the ocean breeze caresses my face on my slow run, I realize something else. When I come back home to face whatever consequences Dad decides to deal out, I don't have to take them. He can do what he wants, but I don't have to listen.

The rhythm of my steps seems to be a drumbeat that's awakening a change in me. I'm done with online classes. I'm not going to learn anything more about cooking, sewing, child development, or whatever is supposed to make me into a suitable wife for someone. I'm going to go to art school. Live and in-person, with other people I can smell, touch, and maybe be friends with. I will sit in a room and revel in the scent of paint and turpentine and clay and create things.

Whatever role Warrick plays in all of that, I don't know. I'm not going to ask him for help, but somehow, I'll figure it out.

I look up, and he's now about thirty paces ahead of me and is heading toward the pond. Warrick turns to watch as I catch up. He jogs in place, a bemused look on his face.

"Oh," I say, out of breath as I approach. "You were serious about the running part."

I can't help myself. My eyes travel down and take in the dark fuzz on his legs below the spandex shorts.

"Of course, I'm serious about running. It's the one habit that will keep my fat ass from dying of a heart attack after retiring," he jokes.

Warrick says this with a laugh, but the idea of this mighty figure being taken down by a heart problem is unnerving, to say the least.

"What do you mean?" I ask.

He's still running in place, but I've stopped.

"I'll most likely be alone, so there won't be anyone to call the paramedics. I'd like to have a fighting chance."

At that image, every one of my internal organs contracts in terror. "Alone? I doubt that very much."

"I live alone now."

"Maybe not for long," I say, then make a loud, shocked noise at my own forwardness, covering my mouth.

He chuckles. "Maybe not."

I pick at the rose bushes that line the trail, smoothing my thumb over the small, serrated leaves, and shake my head. "I shouldn't have said that. I know you were just making conversation at dinner about my future."

Finally, Warrick stops running in place. "I wasn't making conversation. I meant every word. And I meant every word last night. Whatever you want to do, you should do it."

I lift one shoulder. "I wouldn't know where to begin. I've never left the state and never had a job. I don't have a driver's license. Not even a suitcase."

Warrick's look of concern turns graver. "They've never taken you anywhere? Not allowed you to get a license?"

My cheeks heat, but not from shame. The way he words it, the way he looks at me, he's the first person to ever put the onus on my parents and not me. I feel trembly, and my finger pricks on a thorn in the rose bush. "Ouch!" I suck my breath through my teeth and instinctively pull my hand back, securing the thorn deeper. "Ow, ow, ow!"

Warrick's big hand closes over mine to still me. And his other hand gently pulls the stem in the other direction, freeing me from the stabbing.

"Thank you," I say, pulling away. But he doesn't let go. Instead, he lifts my hand to look closer. "You're bleeding, petal."

"It's nothing."

My mouth falls open as I watch the man take my pierced thumb and bring it to his mouth. His lips suction softly over the wound, and I feel his tongue slide over it, licking away the blood. Heat blooms between my thighs, slicking the folds of my pussy. His hand around mine was already too much for my needy body. Seeing and feeling his lips on my finger? His tongue moving ...oh my gosh, my knees may buckle.

He pulls my hand away from his lips and smiles, satisfied that the bleeding has stopped. I don't meet his gaze but watch as his thick, hairy fingers weave through my smaller, paler ones. The brush of skin on skin sends warmth and strength radiating from that hand into mine.

The morning sun beats down on us; the asphalt seems to be causing optical illusions in the air around us. I might be lightheaded, from lust, from humidity, and from the scent of roses.

Laughter and chitchat break through my stupor, and I look back at the opposite end of the street that leads to the golf course. A pair of runners are heading our way. Immediately I feel the panic—as if us being seen together is a bad thing, inherently immoral.

Warrick senses me stiffen and looks over at the trailhead, then pulls me along with him. "Come on, let's run in the shade. There are things I need to tell you."

THIS TIME, hidden in the woods, Warrick runs slowly enough for me to keep up and for us to have a reasonable, if only slightly breathless, conversation.

"What did you have to tell me, Warrick?"

Steam rises from the gravel pathway as more sunlight pours in from the canopy above. The way Warrick holds his arms, and the even strides of his sturdy legs, gives him the look of a sexy rugby player. Though, he moves gracefully as if he's been running for decades.

"This is not easy, but you need to know some things about your father."

I snort. "I know what you think of my father. He's a controlling jerk. Well, you're right."

"Not just that, Colette." Even when speaking about my father, how Warrick says my name sends shivers down my spine. "I did some searching online. I know all about his so-called church. Your father is not ordained by any church that I can find. He does collect tithes for a building fund."

I nod. "Yeah. I know. Why are you telling me all this?"

Warrick is more used to this fitness level and can continue on without gasping. I, on the other hand, am starting to wheeze. We are past the gravel and headed across the causeway toward the beach, and a lovely ocean breeze rejuvenates me.

"Here's the thing. Your father has collected more than enough to build a building, but there's no deed, no bank loans, no permits, blueprints, or plans on record."

"Oh," I say, still confused.

Warrick doesn't want to push me; I can feel it in the charged silence that follows as we pick up our pace for the next few minutes. Both of us seem to have a silent agreement to concentrate on running instead of talking.

I feel bad for how my family and I presented ourselves last night. We gave such a weird impression that, of course, Warrick felt the need to poke around in dad's affairs.

I mull all of this over in my head when we reach Ocean Drive, and I'm dripping with sweat. When I stumble,

Warrick touches my elbow, and I feel I could catch fire at the electricity in his touch. "Are you okay?"

I nod, leaning over to catch my breath, my hands on my knees.

Warrick looks around, then gestures with his chin to a snow cone stand by the public beach access.

"Let's have a refreshment," he says.

Me? I'm looking past him toward the Gulf.

"Sure," I say and take off across the busy crosswalk, but keep walking past the snow cone stand and toward the beach.

"Where are you going, petal?" He's rather brazen with how he calls me by the nickname he's given me right out in public. But there's no one we know here. Mom and Dad never come to the beach, and we're miles from the neighborhood.

"To cool off. Come on!"

He calls after me, but I barely hear him; I'm so focused on getting into the ocean. I can't remember the last time I was here. Never without supervision. I sprint through the surf, jumping with the waves, and squeal at the cool water that the ocean hurls against my frame. I close my eyes, lick the saltwater off my lips, and laugh.

I hear Warrick's footsteps behind me, and I keep going, deeper and deeper, until I'm waist high and completely soaked through.

Turning to face him, he's standing perfectly still in the water, his feet planted on the seafloor below, as sturdy as pilings. He, too, is soaked through his shirt and shorts.

And then, my eyes land on the bulge. Oh, heck. I don't have anything to compare it to apart from the sex videos I've seen. And I know from what Lily has told me, those guys are sometimes made to look bigger than they are, or are, uh, "special." Warrick, it seems, is not just unique. He's...gifted. Each time a large wave approaches and the seawater is momentarily sucked away, I glimpse his clinging shorts, now wet and showing quite the log resting against his inner thigh.

"I have to tell you something," I say, swiping the saltwater out of my face, still catching my breath both from the running and from working up the nerve to say what I want to say.

"Yes?"

Competing with the wind and surf, my words become more high-pitched, earnest, and embarrassingly bossy. "You think you're alone? I'm alone! I've always been alone! In my thoughts, in the way that I think about things. And I'm sick of it! I don't want to be alone anymore, and I don't want you to die alone so...so...what do we do now?"

After a long pause in which Warrick stares at me, he gives me the answer. "We put one foot in front of the other."

"Like this?" I take one step forward, reaching for Warrick. At that moment, I see his hands reaching out for me...just as a powerful wave knocks me right under the water.

EIGHT

Warrick

THANK God this woman can swim because she certainly cannot stand up in the ocean. Not without my help. And I'm more than happy to hold on to her.

I help Colette to her feet and guide her closer to shore. The surf knocks her down again and again. Both of us laughing, exhausted by the time we reach a manageable patch of sand, she shouts, "Oops," and falls once again, pulling me down with her.

I believe she might have done that on purpose, but I'm not going to call her out on it. Colette can do whatever she wants as far as I'm concerned. As the surf threatens to overtake her where she lies, I find myself hovering over top of her, cradling her head in my two hands. The surf splashes over my shoulders, but my Colette remains unharmed.

We both seem to realize at the same time that I'm nestled between her legs in the sand. Wordless and with a sort of wonderment in our eyes, we study each other's faces for what seems like an eternity. Her mist gray eyes barely contain her wide-open curiosity that draws out every protective instinct from me. She's too trusting, and I wonder what she sees in me. I've seen too much. I know too much. I'm too old, too experienced, too everything for this woman. Yet there's no way I'm letting her free of this embrace without kissing her.

Soft skin rakes up the outside of my calf, her foot rubbing against me. At the same time, her eyes widen, and her nostrils flare. Even she cannot believe she's given herself permission to do what she's doing.

My lips descend on hers in a wet, soft, saltwater kiss. A chaste kiss. I resist the temptation to spear my tongue inside her mouth the way I want to. It's only the melding of lips, and yet I feel her exhale dreamily. God, she's so sweet; she clenches my heart. I do not deserve such an adorable, charming young woman.

"Warrick."

I press another small kiss to her lips, teasing, my beard dripping saltwater all over her chin.

"Colette."

Her eyes flash at hearing me say her name, and she raises her head, begging for more of me. Cupping her head firmly, I make the next kiss longer, licking the outside of her lip with my tongue. Not pushing in but merely testing, tasting. The sensation I give her draws out the smallest of moans, and I realize this much kissing, out here in public, was a mistake. My cock has gone rock hard between her legs.

This is the sheltered daughter of a sketchy pastor. Whether or not he's on the up and up, that doesn't change who she is. Go slowly, man. Don't fuck it up.

There is zero chance I will be able to hide my erection

when I stand. I've just got to brass my way through it, knowing there's not a man in sight who wouldn't react the same way when kissed by a softly moaning Colette Roberts. Assisting her to her feet, the thought of anyone else popping a stiffy in reaction to this woman makes me utterly insane with a new territorial rage. I glance up and down the beach quickly, irrationally on the lookout for other people staring at my wet-shirted babe. Pull yourself together, Warrick.

"We'd better head back," I say. "You've been gone a long time. I don't want anyone to worry."

As I watch Colette bite her bottom lip, fighting the feelings that both flooded our senses a moment ago, my heart cracks open.

I grasp her chin with my thumb and forefinger. "Bide your time. Be a good girl. You just had a momentary need to rebel and go for a run today; that's all anyone needs to know."

"I hate it there. It's my prison. I don't want to go back." Her lips tremble, and I almost lose it. I have to fight the urge to do what I want to: whisk her away from whatever half-life she's been living. Take care of her, show her the whole world she's been missing. But it's not time yet.

I smile. "Not anymore, it's not. Now you know you can leave. You're free to go and do and be whoever you want. But you have to go about it the right way. I'm going to help you. Will you let me help you?"

She nods, but she can't hide the worry.

I lean over and press another kiss to her soft, welcoming lips, swiping my tongue over her mouth.

"When we return to the woods, we're just neighbors who happened to meet up on our morning run and struck up a conversation."

"Okay." She's being brave for me.

Pressing a kiss to the tip of her perky nose, I give her the only assurance I can at this point.

"I'll see you tonight."

"When we return to the woods, we're just neighbors who happened to meet up on our morning run and struck up a conversation."

"Okay." She's being brave for me.

Pressing a kiss to the tip of her perky nose, I give her the only assurance I can at this point.

"I'll see you tonight."

NINE

Colette

INSTEAD OF GOING to my studies, I breeze through the living room where my stressed-looking father sits at his computer. I ignore his stern looks, blowing right past him into the kitchen, where I grab myself some water.

As expected, he follows me. I'm not worried. I just had my first kiss, and it was a thousand times more romantic and thrilling than I had ever expected it to be.

"And just where did you disappear to, Colette Elizabeth?"

Uh oh. He's using my middle name.

I don't answer until after taking a gulp of water. I swipe the back of my sweaty arm over my lips and exhale in relief at the water quenching my thirst. "I went for a run like I said."

"You were supposed to be in sewing class an hour ago," he says.

"Oh, right," I say, brushing past him where he stands

with his hands on his hips. I pad over to the pantry and quickly examine it for snacks. My mother only stocks healthy stuff like kale chips and granola, but I manage to find some Blueberry Chex cereal—about as good as it will get for junk food in this house. "I'm not doing sewing anymore." I fill a bowl, set it on the marble countertop, and go back to the stainless steel fridge to fetch the half and half.

"That's not an option. Our house, our rules," he says, ogling the milk I'm pouring over my cereal. "And that's full of cream; that's not good for your figure, Colette."

I think poor old Jarvis's brain is shorting out because he doesn't know which sin to scold me about.

I shrug. "You'll get over it."

Behind me, Mom makes a startling yipping noise as she closes the door to the backyard where she's been tending her garden, probably. "Colette! We don't speak to your father that way."

With a mouth full of delicious cereal, I spin around and say, "Hey, Mom! You look sweaty. Let me get you some water."

"I'm fine," she says, pulling off her gardening gloves. "But we need to talk about this...this sudden need to rebel."

I cock my head and munch my cereal. "It's not that interesting. Instead, how about we talk about me not taking any more online classes? Except for maybe art. Sketching, painting, maybe writing!"

Grace shakes her head. "I just don't know what has brought this on."

"Maybe the fact that I'm 22?"

Grace looks past me, and I see her exchange a knowing look with Dad.

I slurp down the rest of my cereal, rinse out the bowl in the sink and place my bowl and spoon in the dishwasher.

Mom and Dad, weirdly, haven't said anything else to me. So, I assume this discussion is over. I grab my water bottle and float into the library to peruse a book to read. When they don't follow, I examine my mother's section. I don't know why I never noticed romance books before. My hands run over the spines of several that, when I take them out, contain Amish characters on the cover. I pick one up that looks interesting. Farther along the rows, however, I spot one with its spine facing in, and page edges out. Curious, I tug on the book, which has been tightly wedged in between two cozy mysteries. I stare agog at the cover, which features a shirtless man leaning over a prone woman whose dress seems moments away from giving up any pretense of covering her ample bosoms. I am instantly aroused. The woman's hair is splayed out over lush pillows, and the expression on her beautiful face indicates she's either in great pain or in the throes of a religious experience. The man's back muscles are bunched as if he's ready to thrust into the woman, ravishing her thoroughly, except those pesky trousers are in the way.

Grinning, I tuck the book under my arm and make my way outside to the back deck.

I can't wait to read whatever it is that my mother has been hiding from my father.

TEN

Warrick

THE WOMAN HAS POSSESSED ME.

That kiss was not enough.

I trudge up to my room and slap my wet clothes into the hamper, barely glancing around my barren, gray bedroom. Just yesterday, I was content in this space. I'd hired a designer to customize the house to my exact specifications. I never needed a man cave; everywhere I look is a man cave but with expensive taste. How the designer was able to incorporate Floridian pastels into a masculine vibe, I don't know. Nor do I care. I command Alexa to turn on the rain showerhead to my preset temperature and glance around at the bathroom. This house was to be my retirement haven. I would spend the next few years gradually doing fewer and fewer consultant jobs, spacing those jobs out between rounds of golf, and swimming in my own private garden pool. Be alone and content to read, write, run, and travel whenever the urge struck me. I never even wanted a dog to tie me down, let alone another person.

Until now.

The shower streams over my face, washing away the sweat and saltwater, but nothing can wash away the taste of sweet Colette on my lips.

I never thought this would be me. I never pictured myself as someone's much-older lover. All my life, I'd laughed at sugar daddies and how foolish they were to be taken advantage of.

But now, I'm beginning to understand it. I haven't spent a dime on this girl, but she has me already feeling an odd thrill at the idea of paying for her education. Paying for new clothes, a car, whatever the hell she wants.

I use the overpriced natural loofah that my housekeeper keeps stocked in the shower to suds up my skin, scrubbing away the sweat and dirt from my run.

There's one key difference between a sugar daddy and what I expect from Colette. I don't want to put her up in an apartment or a house by herself. I want her to live with me and me alone. As my wife.

The memory of her lips on mine, her hands on my chest, fills me with so much passion that I cannot contain it. No one has ever affected me this way. I slide my palm down my torso and find my hardened cock begging for relief. Gritting my teeth, I prop myself against the tile with one hand and wrap my other hand around my length, sliding it through my fist. I close my eyes and see her face. I memorized it the second I first laid eyes on her. Colette. She's turned everything upside down in the best way.

I pump myself and think of her kiss, her smile, the way she says my name. How she looked so sad when I tried to turn down dinner, then the way she lit up when I accepted. Her eagerness and interest in our dinner conversation.

By the time I finish, and the shower drain washes away all traces of my spend, I feel enough relief to take the edge off my anxiety. It's just enough to let me think clearly.

I have to do this the right way. We have to be discreet. I have to protect her reputation. But sooner rather than later, Colette must get away from those people.

ELEVEN

Colette

I READ UNDISTURBED ALL DAY, occasionally stopping to swim in the pool. At some point, I email Candace, who, to my delight, agrees right away to come over and join me for a swim. I feel like a teenager on summer vacation, lounging by the pool and doing nothing. Is this what summers are like in ordinary families? Is this what friends do?

"You know," Candace says, "I don't think I've ever been inside your house before."

We sip our lemonade, and I think about that.

"You're right," I say, knowing that I've only ever been over to Candace's house, maybe once or twice. Not since middle school, when we used to have sleepovers with the other little girls in the neighborhood.

I swallow hard because I want to tell her the truth. "I wonder if we'd be better friends if my dad had never started that church. He just ... doesn't like me hanging out with anyone other than people who he personally vets. I'm sorry."

She nods thoughtfully. I wait for her to say something critical. I wait for her to ask why I never stood up to my parents. Instead, she sips her lemonade through her pink straw and casually says, "Man, that sucks. I'm sorry they did that to you."

I'm stunned.

"Thank you," I rasp, a hard knot forming in my throat.

She looks over her shoulder. "So, why are they not making a fuss about me being here now?"

I shrug. "I'm not sure. They've been stressed all day, taking phone calls from the bank and some guy from church. All the better, less attention on me when they're so preoccupied. They haven't said anything about me going running with the new neighbor. They were surprised and shocked, but they didn't stop me, and they haven't spoken to me since."

Candace sits forward in her seat and sets down her glass. "Wait a minute. The new neighbor? Hottie McBeardface?"

A heat that has nothing to do with the Florida sun creeps over my skin. "He does have a beard."

Candace nearly jumps out of her seat. "Dude!"

I'm feeling extremely self-conscious now. "What?"

She looks around furtively and then makes a strange noise like a combination of an animal woof, a scoff, and a goat's bleat. She points in the direction of Warrick's house. "That man is the only topic of gossip among the housewives at the club."

"He is?"

"And you went running with him?"

"Yes?" I say meekly.

"How did that happen?" She excitedly stomps her bare feet on the concrete patio.

I sigh and try to decide how to quickly bring her up to speed. I suppose it's all going to come out sooner or later. So I tell her everything.

"Girl," is all she says.

I cover my face with my hand, blushing hard now.

"Is that all?" Candace asks.

"No?"

"Colette! Tell me!"

"We might have kissed. A lot. On the beach. After falling down and pulling him on top of me... and it might have also been my first kiss."

"Whoa."

"I know. I know! He's 52. It looks fucked up, but I swear—"

Candace reaches across and grabs my hand. "No, honey. No. That's not what I'm freaking out about."

"You're not?"

"No. My parents have a twenty-year age gap; she used to be a yacht girl; it was a whole thing. No, I don't give a fuck about that. I am freaking out because I'm in shock. You never leave the house, and now you're gonna get the most sought-after D in the neighborhood!"

It doesn't seem possible that I could blush any harder, but I do. At the same time, I look down at our joined hands and realize that no girl, no woman, no friend in my life has ever shown me this type of physical affection. It's nice.

I am not going to let myself get mushy right now, though. Having a friend over is too much fun.

Mischievously I find myself asking, "What are they saying about him at the club?"

Candace arches an eyebrow and says, "Mrs. Waterford

has been harboring fantasies of blowing him on the 18th hole."

I bark out a laugh, but the thought of this sets my teeth on edge. And those teeth may as well have fangs because the next thing I feel is...homicidal.

I have no claim on Warrick, and yet so much fire in my belly, it wouldn't surprise me if my eyes could shoot lasers and burn Mrs. Waterford's house to the ground from where I sit.

TWELVE

Warrick

CLOSING out my browsers and email inboxes, I decide I've seen all the proof I need about the people next door. Now, I just have to figure out how to tell Colette everything I've learned today.

I switch off my light, strip down and lie back on the bed. Besides reconnaissance work, I've managed to get some writing done on my book. And yes, I did it while parked next to my window, just waiting for a glimpse of my sweet girl.

It's late now, and her bedroom is still dark. Maybe she's changed her mind.

Eventually, distant thunder and the rain pattering against my window lull me into a fitful sleep.

Hours later, a shaft of light pierces through my bedroom window. The rain has abated. Colette is awake.

I sit up in bed and look over. I can just make out her form, padding around her pale yellow bedroom, dressed in a thin summer bathrobe. She pauses at the window and looks out into the darkness. The damp night air is full of the trilling of crickets and insanely loud cicadas. Her window pane is lifted, and her bedroom curtains sway in the night breeze. I stay frozen. She bites her lip first. Then, a slow smile tugs at the corner of her mouth.

Curious, I watch her disappear deeper into the room. When I fully open my window, I hear water running. She's showering.

I sit forward on the edge of the bed, my lower half illuminated by the light from her window.

When Colette emerges from the shower, I expect her to wear that robe again. But she's bare-ass naked to the world, and my entire body hums at the sight of her. She's wet, dripping water all over her floors.

Then, something happens I never could have anticipated from this pure, innocent soul. She pauses in front of the window, displaying herself to me. I drink it all in. Her hair has been towel-dried and clings to her neck and shoulders. Droplets are scattered over her chest, her perky, round breasts. I am drooling like a dog. Her hands slowly drift down below her navel, across her bare pussy. I hold my breath as she tortures me with this vision.

This is happening too fast for her. This is my fault. I woke this up in her.

I have to think. I have to plan. We have to wait for the right time. We have to talk this through.

But all the have-tos and shoulds leave my brain the second her delicate fingers pinch one nipple. The world I know, all my plans, everything caving in on itself.

THIRTEEN

Colette

RISING from the end of the bed, Warrick adjusts himself. His erection rests upright against his lower stomach, the waistband of his boxer briefs cutting across its width.

My stomach erupts in butterflies. I'm going to see a whole penis for the first time ever.

He approaches the window, one hand casually massaging his hard length up and down. I echo his movements but with long strokes up and down my breasts, massaging moisturizer into my skin. This is...not that different from what I usually do when I get out of the shower. I'm just letting him watch.

"Come closer to the window, Colette. Come close and let me see you."

My breath hitches as I watch him stroke the underside of his thickness through the material.

I obey, and my heart thuds against my sternum as I come closer. I lick my lips, wishing I could kiss him.

Warrick grips the window frame and leans forward as if somehow we can reach each other through the windows. We're not even close enough to share air, but my body is compelled forward.

I can't get much closer, so I kneel on my window seat, spreading my legs wide.

"Do you want to see it, Colette?"

Thunder rumbles and a gentle rain begins again. Hopefully, the weather won't disrupt...whatever we're doing here.

"Y-yes. Please."

Warrick disappears for a second, then comes back, completely naked. The shaft stands erect and free, and for the first time, I realize that he might be too big for me.

I watch, agape, while Warrick pumps his thick length up and down. He starts slowly at first, letting me take it all in small doses.

"Don't stop, petal. Let me watch you pleasure yourself."

My breath shudders as need rolls through me. His groan is audible as my hand dips down and my fingers part my folds.

"That's it, sweetheart."

I squeak and bite down on my lip as my finger sinks deeper. My clit is a hard, angry nub.

"Good girl. Now spread your legs wider, and let me see you play."

Heat flashes across my face. But I do as he says as the rain falls harder. I can't believe we're doing this. We'll be arrested if someone sees.

"I just wish...I just wish it was you. Your hands."

"Soon enough, petal."

Thunder booms as Warrick pumps his rod.

Uncontrollable, desperate noises squeak from my throat.

I am almost to the tipping point, but I hate this. Why did I start this? I don't want to do this without him.

"I want your hands on me, Warrick."

What I don't say is I want to be the one pumping that fat, angry limb for him. Even though I know it's too big, I want it to break me, and I want to ride it until I fall apart.

"Warrick, stop!" I cry, pulling my hands away from my pussy.

He pauses, his chest heaving, his face the picture of need and frustration.

Warrick's thick fingers rest on his hips, his broad upper torso still rapidly rising and falling but a little slower than a minute ago. He glares over at me as if I've caused him pain.

"My god, I could break down your door and rut into you like a man on fire."

The hot flush begins at my feet and rolls over me. "I want that. I want that right now."

"Colette," he growls, the thunder echoing his energy. My nipples harden at this combined sound, the wind and rain now breaching the window and splattering lightly inside my room. The dripping between my legs is comically Pavlovian at this point. I'm so aroused, I shout in my frustration. "And what do you think it's like for me? I have nothing to do but think of you while I'm cooped up here!"

Warrick holds up his hands in surrender. "We have to be discreet. I'm trying to protect your reputation."

My impatience grows, and I have to shout over the sound of the rush of rain and the thunder. I think about what Lily said in our most recent chat. She'd said I was making a huge mistake and that the whole scenario made her ill. So, yes, I know what this relationship will do to my reputation. And I don't care.

"When? When can I get out of here?"

Warrick seethes, both hands clasping the sides of the window, the rain splattering against his naked body.

"Now, Colette. Right fucking now." He motions toward the back of the house. Right. The poolside door.

My heart leaps as I grab a couple of things and head toward the exit.

Only to find my bedroom door locked from the outside.

FOURTEEN

Warrick

HAVING THROWN on a pair of athletic pants, I run out the door to the backyard and dash through the storm to Colette's back patio.

I turn the knob of the door there, but it's deadlocked. I wait under the awning for about a minute, and then I worry. If I check the front door, I might miss her.

Something feels very wrong. Lightning crashes. Maybe she's scared to come outside. As she should be; this is madness.

I try the door one more time, then give up, thinking I'll dash up the alley to the front door and knock. Yes, I'll wake up her parents but at this point, let them try to stop me.

Lightning crashes again while I'm right under her window. I look up, and she's still there, but her bathrobe is tied closed.

"Colette!"

She calls down, barely audible over the sound of the rain, "They locked me in my room!"

"Motherfucker!"

"Stay there!" Colette calls down. "I'm coming!"

I can't fathom what she means.

And then, she's sitting on the window ledge, her legs hanging down.

"No! No, don't jump! Don't do anything crazy!"

A triumphant smile is etched on Colette's face. "I'm already crazy. Now, catch!"

I shout at her to stop. Rain floods my eyes and ears; I don't know if I'll be able to catch her. But does she listen? No.

Colette wildly leaps from the window, falling about fifteen feet, straight into me.

Steeling for the impact, I feel no pain by breaking her fall as she tumbles into me. Rain pelts my face, and I can't see clearly enough to assess any injuries. "Colette, have you lost your mind? Don't ever do that again!"

Her arms circle my neck, and she wrangles her legs around my waist. Her kiss is hard, urgent. "I need you, Warrick. Please don't be upset with me."

How could I be upset with her when her soft mouth begs me to kiss her back? I love her for what she did.

She is the wildest, bravest, most dynamic woman I've ever met, and I am out of my mind for her. She grinds against my body as we kiss in the pounding rain, tongues stabbing, teeth clacking, and desperate moans tumbling from our throats. Her fingers dig into the back of my head, forcing me closer as if she wants to consume me. I know the feeling.

It's madness not to go indoors, but I can't stop touching

her, kissing her, long enough to run to safety. I can't even breathe, and I do not care.

"Petal," I manage to grind out, backing her up against the brick wall. The rain shreds the earth, and the wind howls. I smooth her matted hair out of her pleading eyes, but it's no use; we're half-blinded from the rain.

I pull back from her body, just barely enough to give her some relief. I have to, though. I have to give her what she needs.

Before Colette can protest, I shuck her soaked, flimsy robe out of the way and cup her heat. Colette lets out a soft whimper at this contact. My fingers massage her soft, velvety folds as her eyes close.

"Talk to me, petal."

She hums and nods.

"If you say yes, I'll be fucking you with my fingers. I need to hear the words. Do you want me to keep going?"

That's when her body freezes, and her eyes go wide.

I've pushed her too far, too fast. And now she's having second thoughts. She realizes that 30 years isn't a gap; it's a chasm.

Her wide eyes stare back at me in fright, and I'm sure I've just lost everything.

FIFTEEN

Colette

HE'S SLOWING.

No, he's stopping.

Why is he stopping?

My eyes fly open, my body still on fire with desire. Warrick's hand still holds my pussy, but he's not...doing that thing...that thing that made my eyes roll back in my head.

Is he having second thoughts?

"Tell me what you're thinking, Colette. Use words."

What I'm thinking? I have no thoughts, only feelings.

My body grinds against his hand, and I squeak. "The only word I have for you is yes!" I cry out as lightning crashes, and something cracks open not far from us. The world trembles around us, and I think a tree must have fallen.

Relief floods his face, followed by fresh determination. Warrick sinks the tip of his finger into my passage while his thumb toys with my clit.

How...how does he do that?

Simultaneous sensations drive my pleasure to a new level. I have to hold on tighter while my body automatically falls into a rhythm against his hand, riding it. Angling for more pressure, more contact.

My hands caress all of Warrick's delicious bare skin within reach. His broad chest, thick shoulders. Mine. All mine.

A second finger joins the first inside my pussy, and the feeling of fullness is surprising and delightful. And yet he's also taunting, playing with my clit. I need...what do I need?

Something between a snarl and a whimper escapes me; I may combust if he continues to impale me and stretch me like this.

And then it happens. His thumb moves over my throbbing button. A direct hit, and I come apart.

My nails dig into his shoulders, and I have to keep from biting down on his tongue inside my mouth.

I pull away from him then, reeling from the intensity of this orgasm.

"Colette. Colette. Petal." He croons sweet words as I go limp in his arms.

We might as well get struck by lightning because I feel like I just lived my entire life in the last five minutes.

SIXTEEN

Warrick

HOW FUCKING DARE those people try to lock up my girl. Colette.

Now that we're safely inside my house while the storm rages on outside, we see each other clearly.

I don't care that we're leaving a trail of mud and rainwater or that my entire house has never seen a speck of dirt. Together, Colette and I strop off our wet clothes and chuck them in the washer, laughing at how we look like a pair of drowned rats.

Although in truth, she looks just as wild, beautiful, and sexy as she did a minute ago. The recent memory of Colette grinding against me in the middle of an electrical storm has my cock rising once again.

All of her, the complete package, has turned me inside out. It's not just her nakedness but her everything. Her sweetness, her curiosity, her radiance ... her scent. *That* scent.

Colette's wide eyes dip down, spying my throbbing cock.

"Oh my," she breathes. "Sorry to...keep you waiting."

I love how my girl blushes. I pull her close to me and speak softly against her rain-soaked hair. "There's time for that later," I tell her.

"But...does it not...hurt?" Her soft hand travels down my chest and over my stomach, stopping just shy of the tip. "Do you want me to..."

She can't hide the embarrassment in her tone. I hate what people have done to make her feel uncomfortable talking about these things.

I shake my head no. "That's the advantage of fucking a man my age. I've learned how to enjoy that ache and make it last."

Colette blinks several times in surprise and shock. "Oh...okay."

"And besides, I have more important business to attend to."

"You have?"

I nod slowly. "I'm hungry, and I want your scent on me."

Her body trembles in my arms. "You...want my scent?"

God, she doesn't know how good she smells. Nor does she understand what I want, so I have to be more straight-forward.

"Let me taste you, Colette. I want to put my mouth on your pussy and make you come."

I take full advantage of her small open-mouthed gasp, peppering kisses everywhere, capturing each lip between mine in rapid succession, licking her mouth and teeth and tongue until she's breathless.

"I've...never...."

"I know. I'll show you what I mean. In the bedroom."

And still, we can't stop kissing and touching and teasing each other's trembling, naked bodies until we're both worked up into a frenzy.

"Oh...I understand..." she murmurs against my mouth. "You want me to sit on your face."

Holy shit.

She giggles. "I have seen that sort of thing before. Just be patient because I don't know what to do."

I can't help myself, and I plunge my tongue into her mouth and claim her pussy with my hand again. "All you have to do is let go and let me take control. That's all you have to do."

SEVENTEEN

Colette

I MAY GO blind with the pleasure of Warrick's face and beard under me...between my legs, between the folds of my pussy.

I wondered if I would like this. Sure, in all those videos, the women look like they enjoy oral, but that's acting. But now, I get it.

How could I have doubted that this thick, soft beard wouldn't take me for the ride of my life? Not to mention his outrageously sensuous mouth.

"Oh, god," I croon. My knees are planted on the mattress on either side of Warrick's head, and I'm clutching the headboard so tight that the carved wood digs into my hands. The pain in my fingers only adds to the pleasure surging through me. Every sensation heightens my body's awareness.

His tongue spears into me, licking my inner walls. I

needn't have worried that I wouldn't know what to do; everything below the waist moves on its own.

The wet noises make me curse — and I barely know how to curse. Every sound and movement draws out more wetness from my dripping cunt.

I love this so damn much I want to grind, but I fear I might suffocate the poor man.

He seems to be breathing just fine, though. Warrick's moans vibrate against my sensitive skin, making me gasp and cry out in shock.

Something takes hold of me, and I feel myself growing wild and desperate for release.

I come up on my knees, and I'm overcome by my lover's face and his beard slick with my essence.

"Warrick," I squeak. "I...I need...well, I don't know what I need...I...."

He laughs. This devil between my thighs laughs. "I know what you need, petal."

"P-please?"

"Do you trust me?"

I nod. "Always and forever."

EIGHTEEN

Warrick

ROLLING HER UNDERNEATH ME, I give her all I have.

My mouth suctions against her clit, two fingers push into her yielding cunt, and a third digit softly explores the tight spot between her cheeks. I cannot get enough of my darling girl.

The stroking and the suction transport my Colette to her second orgasm of this wild and unexpected night. "Warrick! Yes! Oh my god, yes!"

She doesn't hesitate when I hold her tight to kiss her and caress her through her aftershocks.

She trembles and gives a small laugh after she calms. "Now I understand what all the fuss is about!"

We laugh together. Both of us are shocked and amused at how perfectly matched we are.

And despite my stamina, I need to be inside her. Now.

"I love you, Colette. I need you with me. Now, tomorrow, and the next day. I want to put my baby in you. Now. Right now. I'm aching. So bad. May I, please, Colette?"

She smiles a radiant smile, touches my cheek, and then kisses me softly. "Will you love me always and forever?"

I nod.

"Will you show me how? I...don't know if I know how to love...or take care of someone. I can barely take care of myself."

I push in, her tightness hugging me hard. "You already have made me feel loved. You've already made me feel like a king, petal."

Colette hooks her feet together at the small of my back and guides me in, all the way to the hilt.

"Oh fuck...fuck me, you're so wet and tight."

I keep my eyes trained on hers, watching for signs of pain.

"I'm ok," she says, anticipating my concerns. "It doesn't hurt. You feel wonderful."

We build a comfortable, loving rhythm.

I surge into her, filling her with my cum, roaring her name amidst a string of curses I would never normally speak in her presence.

Colette's tight cunt bears down, pulling everything out of me, drawing out every ounce of pleasure and seed from me.

I stay nested inside her tight warmth and roll her on top of me. The world has disappeared for this blissful hour, and it's starting to creep back in.

Colette senses it, too.

"Was there something you wanted to tell me?"

Now we come to the part I've been dreading.

NINETEEN

Colette

"SWEETHEART, I'm sure there's a logical explanation. Are you sure your friends aren't jumping to conclusions?"

At Warrick's sleek kitchen table, my lover has just spent the last twenty minutes telling me my father, a church pastor and a pillar of the community, is a crook.

He's shown me his email thread with contacts who know him. None of this makes any sense to me.

"I've known my father to be a harsh disciplinarian, but I've never known him to be a liar or a thief, Warrick."

The words come out a little harsher than I'd meant to. Why am I sticking up for my father, though? Am I biased because I'm his flesh and blood?

I turn Warrick's laptop screen back toward him and wrap my hands around the mug of coffee in Warrick's kitchen, where I sit snuggled in a soft blanket and one of his dress shirts. I'm surrounded by his spicy scent, and it floods me with excitement and pure bliss.

Warrick reaches across the table and rests his hand around mine, which holds the steaming mug. This man has made me feel like a new person in one night. Bonus points for being an excellent cook and serving my favorite breakfast: blueberry pancakes with whipped cream. I feel good in this house. I feel settled and safe when I'm close to him.

I just need to go home and fetch a few things. Explain things to my parents and give them time to settle down before I move out.

"For the record, I hate this idea," Warrick says when I bring up the idea again of telling my parents by myself.

"Don't be silly; I'm just going to go over there and explain what's going on. And I want to rescue my laptop. My art, my whole life—apart from you—are on there."

Although, to be honest, I didn't mind taking a break from checking in with Lily on the Discord server as I usually do every night. We had a few exchanges during the day yesterday that didn't sit right with me. She practically yelled at me over the internet. I don't need that kind of negativity in my life. If she comes around, fine. If not, I guess we're at an impasse.

Candace was accepting of the idea of Warrick and me together. If we get married...when we get married... Candace is the first person on my guest list for the wedding.

Wedding planning. Yet another reason I need to go and get my laptop. Excitement flutters through me at the idea of choosing flowers and a dress, even if it's for a small ceremony.

"So let me go and fetch your laptop. I can have the conversation with your parents," he urges.

I snort. "That won't go well. Besides, do you feel comfortable picking out clothes, and the art supplies I need, during this...time of transition?"

The phrase doesn't sit well in my mouth; it feels like I'm talking about a bank transaction.

Warrick grunts. "I can get you new clothes and art supplies."

Chuckling, I peel his fingers away from mine to give him a squeeze with both of my hands.

"That's so wasteful. Just let me handle it. I owe them a conversation," I say.

He squints slightly. He doesn't want to push, and he can't disagree.

"Then let me go with you. I'm an excellent negotiator."

I stand up and go to him, sliding into his lap. Warrick slips one hand underneath the hem of the shirt I'm wearing. The blanket falls to the floor, but I don't mind. His palm on my middle warms me better than anything. "Negotiator? I'm not a prize heifer, you know." I say it teasingly, leaning down to kiss the spot where the scruff on his jaw meets his ear...and making sure the dress shirt gapes open just enough to distract him from the dark place his mind went to.

It works, and Warrick adjusts me in his lap. His hand travels north to cup my breast.

"You're not?" Warrick asks with a wry smile. "What kind of heifer are you, then? I'll have to talk to the people who sold you to me because I specifically asked for a prized one." He squeezes my tit, and I squeal, wiggling in his lap.

"Keep squirming like that, and I'll be forced to take you back to the bedroom," he says, his breath wafting across the skin of my chest as he kisses my sternum. Warrick's hard length presses into my thigh.

Oops. I've gone too far to distract him now. I muster all my strength to extract myself from Warrick's lap and walk to the dryer to fetch my bathrobe. I take it out, look at it, and think about what comes next. Turning back to him, he's watching my every move from the kitchen like an overprotective bear. Sheepishly, I hold the bathrobe up to my chin and ask, "I don't suppose you have any athletic wear I can throw on for this task? Although I enjoy prancing around in your button-up shirt, it's probably not suitable for outside the house."

Grudgingly, Warrick rises to fetch me his smallest pair of shorts and a Miami Dolphins tee-shirt. He somberly walks away while I get dressed. I'm swimming in this tee shirt and shorts, but they will have to do. I'm not a tiny woman, but I still feel like I'm playing dress-up in this larger-than-life man's clothes.

"This will have to do; thank you."

"Don't go," he tries again.

"Warrick. It's something I have to do. They're probably wondering where I am. I would not be surprised if they called the police by now."

"I don't trust that guy."

"That guy is my dad...and...." I trail off when my mind goes blank. And what? He deserves respect? This is some rite of passage you have to go through?

"You said you trusted me, always and forever." Ok, that stings a little. I search Warrick's face for some kind of emotion other than frustration. I need some sort of tenderness to build me up before I do what I have to do.

"That's not what this is about. I do trust you. With me."

Warrick takes a step forward. "Then you need to trust me that I know what I'm talking about and that keeping you away from them is protecting you."

What exactly does he think he's protecting me from? My palms come together like I'm subconsciously pleading now. "And you aren't trusting me right now. Frankly, I'm a tiny bit hurt. This is a family matter, and I need you to let me handle it."

I don't want to leave Warrick's house, my refuge, in a huff. But I am feeling a little bit prickly.

His eyes bore into me as I turn away and head out the door.

I just have to put one foot in front of the other, past the rose bushes from his driveway to theirs.

The emails he showed me stick in my mind. Warrick's contacts in the city government seem to think Daddy might be embezzling money but then again...maybe there's a better explanation.

My dad has old-fashioned ideas about money and thinks women shouldn't have to worry about those things. I whole-heartedly disagree, but just because I disagree doesn't mean he's a criminal.

And sure, they locked me in my bedroom. But I'm sure that was a temporary overreaction.

I walk into my parents' home, absolutely sure that we'll have a civilized conversation. There's no one in the living room, though. I hear people talking in the kitchen.

On the kitchen table, there is my laptop. It's open to Discord, and my father is scrolling through my entire history of conversations with Lily. Next to my computer is my sketchbook, and it's open to a page with sketches of Warrick.

My head explodes. "What are you guys doing?!"

Dad turns to me. "We thought you'd run away, so we searched through your browser history. We were worried." Oops. Last night before I went to Warrick, I was so keyed up and preoccupied that I'd forgotten to clear my history.

If I was really MIA in their eyes, they're not jumping

up and down with relief that I'm back. "Don't anyone put out an APB on me. I'm fine," I say sarcastically.

Dad gestures at the screen. "Yes. We figured out pretty quickly where you were."

My dad levels me with a gaze that would have sent me spiraling with shame and fear just a few days ago. "All you had to do was move out if that's what you wanted. You don't have to give away the greatest gift a woman has to offer just to get a little bit of freedom."

Happily, his gaze has zero effect on me today. But his words feel like lies, and my hackles go up. Greatest gift? Really? I think everyone here knows if I walked out the door on my own, they would have cut me off, and I would have no clue what to do with myself. I would be on the streets.

I steel myself. Here we go. Too nervous to sit down, I steady myself on the back of the empty chair and take a deep breath. "We need to talk. In light of everything that's happened...."

Mom scoffs. "If you mean whoring yourself to a man old enough to be your grandfather and making a laughingstock of your father, then yes, we need to talk."

I take a step backward. I've never heard my mother use that word toward me. I'm not going to do the math, but I know Warrick's not old enough to be my grandfather. But it's irrelevant. I will be mature. I will be calm. What is relevant to this conversation is they are unhappy, but they need to know they'll get over it.

"Mom. Dad. I'm 22 years old, and I can make my own decisions. I've decided to just come by this morning to grab some clothes and things, and I'll be on my way. I'll be back to collect the rest of my things and have a civil discussion after everyone has calmed down."

Dad crosses his arms over his chest. "You won't be back,

ever. You couldn't sow your wild oats in the city, outside of our knowledge? You had to do it here, right next door, for everyone to see?"

Don't say it, Colette. Don't say the thing you want to say right now. "I guess I could have taken your lead and tried playing footsie with him under the table." Yeah, Warrick told me about that. I shouldn't be so petty, but here we are.

Mom splutters and denies it. Dad turns a venomous look toward her, then back to me.

I need to defuse this ticking time bomb. "Look at it this way; when we start a family, you'll be right next to your grandchildren. Who wouldn't want that?"

Mom and Dad exchange a look. "Correction. We won't be living next door to a devil like that. We're moving...I mean, the *church* is moving us to Costa Rica. To be missionaries."

I scoff. "Taking a missionary job is a bit of a dramatic exit to distance yourself from me, don't you think?"

Something clicks, then. Yes, it is more than a bit dramatic. So dramatic it sounds like ... a lie. But then, there have been a lot of church-related phone calls lately. And mail. Maybe ... maybe this has been in the works for a while?

No, it doesn't add up. I would have heard about a missionary assignment if they were discussing it.

Everything that Warrick warned me about? Now makes the most sense.

"But the building fund...you're supposed to start construction next year?"

Dad glowers at me and doesn't respond.

The sound of the front door opening and closing has everyone's head swiveling toward the living room. Warrick's heavy footsteps approach and my body is flooded with relief.

"You were taking too long. I got worried."

He slips one hand around my waist, and I smile at him.

"She's made it clear what she plans to do. Now, if you'll excuse us," my dad says, too hastily, closing my laptop and tucking it under his arm.

I'm eyeing my laptop. They saw the emails that Warrick forwarded to me. They don't care about me; they just want my computer.

"Don't you...want to have a family meeting, now that I'm permanently in your daughter's life?" Warrick asks.

Mom croaks, "If you don't mind, we have packing of our own to do. So if you could hurry up...."

My mind is reeling. "Today? You all are leaving for Costa Rica today? This is so extreme!"

No one says anything.

Two seconds later, the doorbell rings. Everyone but me and Warrick jumps.

"Who's that?" Mom asks. She looks terrified.

"Why don't you go answer the door and find out?" Warrick says.

Mom looks at Dad. "Jarvis?"

Dad grunts and rises from his chair, glaring at Mom. "Grace. Don't say a goddamn word."

I gasp and cover my mouth. I've never heard my father talk like that, ever.

I look up at Warrick, and his eyes are so full of tenderness and care for me that I can't look away.

At least, not until I hear who it is at the door.

A certain somber bass perks up my ears. "Jarvis?"

"It's Mitch, the church president. What's he doing here?" I ask. Mom looks suddenly pale. Warrick squeezes me close. "I'm so sorry, sweetheart." He kisses the side of my head, and a warm, secure feeling sweeps through me. I don't know what's happening, but I can face it.

In the living room, Dad's whole mood changes in a snap. "Mitchell. I'm so sorry, the wife and I were about to leave ... for a hospital visit. Can this wait until Monday?"

More lies. Warrick was right about everything.

"I'm afraid not. Sit down. The council will be here shortly, and we will have an emergency meeting."

"Oh dear lord," Mom whispers.

All I know is that I don't want to be here for whatever is happening.

I look up at Warrick, and he immediately gets it. And this right here is why he's mine.

TWENTY

Colette

THE AIR HAS CHANGED when we leave my parents'
house. The wet soup atmosphere of Florida in July seems to
have relented.

As we walk through the opening in the hedge between
our two houses, I slip my hand in Warrick's. We don't speak
yet; I think both of us are processing what we just saw and
heard, and we're enjoying the silence. The birds chirping.
The bellowing of toads in the creek. When I touch his hand,
he looks down at me with tenderness.

But then he lets go to softy press his hand to my lower
back and guide me through the hedge in front of him. He's
got my back. This small gesture lifts my spirits after everything that has just happened.

"Are you okay?"

I shrug. "Just feeling a little shaky."

The sensation of his hand on my back warms me and
settles my spirit.

Moments later, he's guiding me upstairs to his bedroom.

"Why don't you lie down and rest. We can hide out here until the storm next door passes," he says, pushing open the door to his room. Or our room. Is it weird for me to call it that already? It feels like my room. It feels like my house.

I sit on the edge of the bed and look at Warrick as he shuts the window and pulls the blind down.

"What's going to happen now?"

Warrick sits next to me on the bed and wraps one big arm around my front, coaxing me to lie down. I give in, and he settles behind me, spooning me and covering me with his warmth and protection.

"Well, they're not going to Costa Rica, that's for sure. The church president could call the police. It's up to those poor folks who donated money to decide."

I think about this, my head spinning with new knowledge. It's as if I never even knew my own family. It was all a facade. It was all part of the plan to look like the perfect, ideal family. It's so much to take that I have to close my eyes and process...until I fall asleep.

When I wake up a few hours later, all I want is comfort. I rotate my body to face Warrick, hooking my thigh around his middle to pull him tight to me.

He hums contentedly and nuzzles my face with his beard. I rub my cheek against his softness—the only thing soft about him, except his tremendous heart, when it comes to me.

His hands caress the length of my spine and then lower down. I sigh and kiss his lips. This revs all his engines, and his touch moves over my cheeks, up and down, and into the split of my rump. I hum into his mouth.

Maybe I shouldn't be in the mood...but why not? I need

this. I need him. My body needs to process this new chapter in my life just as my mind does.

I kiss him harder, and he growls. The vibration of him against my lips is thrilling.

I cry out when he bites down on my lip; he pulls back. "Did I hurt you?"

Nodding, I give him a small smile. "Do it again."

"Oh, Colette. I fucking love you." His words tumble out amidst a deep groan, like a man in pain. I dare say he might be in actual pain.

My hand goes to his middle, and I kiss him back playfully while rubbing that soft area above his waistband. He moans into my mouth when it travels lower, cupping his stiff length through his jogging pants. I rub harder, knowing what's coming next. His cock grows the more I touch it.

"Warrick, I want you to take me hard."

It seems he needs this, too. He's pent up and doesn't know what to do with his energy. Keeping my hand on his dick, I rub harder with the meat of my palm, from the root to the tip. The whole time I do this, I keep my eyes locked on Warrick's. He's so beautiful when he's trying so hard to restrain himself.

"Fuck, Colette. You're going to make me explode. I had no idea you were so wicked."

I lick his bottom lip and nip it with my teeth. "I like to make you want me."

"You don't have to do anything to make me want you. Your existence makes me want to plow you straight through the wall."

I smile. "Do it."

Last night, he took me with such consideration and tenderness that he'd made me sob. Tonight, I want him to unleash on me.

Again, his mouth is on mine, owning me, his greedy tongue demonstrating what he will do to me with his cock. Thrusting, owning, and filling.

It takes no time before he's jerking down my shorts and spreading open my folds with his eager fingers.

He pauses to wriggle out of his shorts and underwear and set his cock free. It's almost like I can hear the thrumming ache between us whenever we're not touching. It's sweet and wonderful and silly and squeezes my heart.

Warrick groans into my mouth, slicking his freed cock between my folds, relishing my lack of underwear. I'm glad he approves. I have loved walking around panty-free. There's something so thrilling about it. It makes me feel wanton and sexy, powerful, and vulnerable. Knowing he could easily take me at any moment has been a fun mind-fuck I've given to myself all day.

Sure beats the daily mind-fuck of feeling unworthy and inadequate.

Even after last night, after everything we did, the noises of him slicking my wetness, using me to lube himself up, make my cheeks heat.

"My petal," he whispers against my lips, the base of his cock tormenting my clit. "Tell me how that feels."

The rubbing of that thick length through my folds, over my clit, is so good I almost can't bear it.

I moan. "Good. So good, Warrick."

The tip swipes against my clit, slowly, then quickly, back and forth, until I'm gasping for air and clawing at Warrick's shoulders.

His voice is low, whispery, and feral as he tortures me with his dick. "You have no idea what I'm going to do to you with this cock, Colette. It's got a mind of its own, and the only thing he ever thinks about is you. Coming back to its sweet, snug little home inside your pussy. Because it's mine. Tell me your pussy isn't aching for me." I feel such a burning, rising pleasure between his words and his wet noises. I need it so badly, but I also feel strong and powerful.

"My...my pussy wants it. Hard. Please," I say.

Warrick snarls, biting my collarbone and then licking the spot.

"It wants to pound you. Own you. Claim you. Do you understand?"

Because I'm breathless and nonverbal now, I nod, rocking my pelvis forward. I just need more touch, more contact, more everything.

I know what he wants, but he first makes me insane with need until I come. Every time we're together, he fills me with the sense that I'm wanted, desired, and cared for.

I come apart at his relentless toying with my tight, hot button. Release washes over me with a half-sob, half-laugh.

"There's my girl. There's my darling girl."

TWENTY-ONE

Warrick

I CANNOT WRAP my mind around how tight, warm, and perfect Colette is. Was she made for me, or vice versa? Maybe both.

Her pussy stretches to fit me and surrounds me tightly as I thrust in and out.

Her soft moans and gasps push me deeper and deeper into my sweet oblivion.

I thrust harder, pushing her up higher and higher on the mattress.

"Take it. Take that dick," I rumble against the supple skin of her throat.

The rougher I am with every retreat and thrust, the tighter her thighs grip me.

I am mad with desire for her. Her body is perfection, but I need more.

Grunting, I impale her on me, hiking up her shirt. Holy

shit, I love railing her hard while she wears my shirt. I need to touch and taste her even as my thrusts grow more frantic.

Her breast is soft and yielding in my hand, and for one wild second, the image of them fuller and round with milk for our baby pops into my head. I seem to grow harder and longer just at the idea of it.

I watch her nipple harden against the swipe of my thumb. I feel the wetness down below increase. Colette's gasping and tightening and rocking back into me makes me unhinged. I cover her nipple with my mouth and lick, suck, tease. I nip her hard bud with my teeth, then pop it out of my mouth to blow on it.

I feel the heat of her desire rise again as her pussy grinds back against me, demanding more.

Her neediness, the way she clings and demands more, always more, makes me feel like a king. I am her king, and she's my queen. I'm going to worship the fucking ground she walks on.

I will give her whatever she wants, and I will mow down anything that stands in her way.

I switch sides and give her other tit the attention it needs, blowing, sucking, playing, and biting.

My touches and tastes have her whimpering, "Yes, please."

My cock doesn't slip out an inch while I lay her back against the pillows and gently take her wrists in my hands. "Reach back and hang on to the headboard, Colette. And hold on tight."

"Yes, Warrick."

God, my name in her mouth is music to my ears.

"Let me hear you keep saying my name while I ram you."

I think I hear a purr, followed by a squeal.

She does exactly as I say. She's so good to me. I'm so fully present inside my own skin with her in my bed.

She makes everything better. Brighter. More fun. More hope-filled and sunny. And at the same time, darker and dirtier.

She has my whole heart. She owns me.

My thrusts slam her so hard that the headboard creaks and slaps against the wall. "Yes. That's it. Take it. Fucking take it. My wife knows how to take that dick."

She mewls, her body coming up off the pillows to take me at every possible angle. "My husband."

The sound of that word coming from her does me in.

With one final, intense press, I explode into my Colette as a roar rips from my throat.

The world goes blank for a second, and everything tightens. My release barrels out of me, filling Colette's pussy with my cum. I come hard and strong, spreading my seed as my hands still her writhing midsection.

Even so, the walls of her sex clamp down tightly. Her insistent grinding ends with her exploding around me in her release. The involuntary spasms of her inner muscles milk me as I continue to jet into her in hard, long spurts.

"That's it, my Colette. Take all of it. Take it all in."

Weakened, her hands let go of the headboard, and her arms wrap around my neck.

While still nestled inside her, I roll onto my back and pull her on top of me.

"Oh!" Colette squeals in surprise and then laughs.

"I like being on top," she says with a giggle.

I'm slick with sweat and our shared release, and nearly out of breath. "We both need to keep up with our running if we're going to survive these vigorous copulations," I say, smoothing her hair away from her face.

"As long as the runs end with us kissing and rolling around on the beach," Colette replies breathlessly, "I'm up for that."

I pepper her forehead with kisses and weave my fingers through her soft hair. "Our public activities might get X-rated. We'll be banned from the beach."

She softly sighs, her breath tickling the hairs on my chest. "We're gonna be shunned from the golf club. Might as well be persona non grata everywhere else."

My stroking hand pauses as this idea sinks in.

I stroke her bare back. "We could always leave."

"Leave? And go where?"

"We could move somewhere where nobody will care about...our differences."

She hums and kisses my chest, then rests her cheek against my skin. Her thumb explores my nipple. "I'm not ashamed. Are you?"

"No. I just wondered."

She lifts her face and crawls up my body to make her gaze even with mine. "People will have to get used to us. We don't have to run away. You just moved in. You like the neighborhood. I love your house, and I have lots of ideas for making it perfect for both of us. I'd like to stay, or at least give it a try."

"You and me against the world, my wife?"

She chuckles. "And here I thought I was the rebel without a cause. It's just you and me; we don't have to be against anything. We can just be."

I squeeze my wife tightly and look forward to when that title is legal and binding. Forever. Because I'm going to give her everything that belongs to me.

She's absolutely right. We have nothing to worry about and nothing to rebel against.

We're not angels, but neither are we devils. We are just two people who found each other by chance and rocked each other's worlds.

The world, such as it is, will carry on.

EPILOGUE

One year later

COLETTE

THE THWACK of the ball against my nine iron is so satisfying. As it sails high and long, I watch past the rolling hills and lands squarely in the sand trap.

"Oh no," I laugh.

"Stay right there," Warrick instructs.

I call after him, "Please don't cheat for me!" But he's already gone, dashing off to retrieve my ball from the sand so that I can hit from the grass.

I'm terrible at golf, but I love golfing with Warrick once a week. He's an excellent, patient teacher. Afterward, we always have lunch at the club. Following that, we go home and shower together. The showering together is my favorite part.

We've already been banned from the locker rooms for

sharing a stall. Nobody saw us, but someone figured it out and complained. Rude.

I giggle as I watch him slide down into the sand trap, my hands blocking the sun from my face when a voice behind me startles me out of my good mood.

"You're certainly working the sugar daddy hard."

I spin around to see Mrs. Waterford, one hand on her hip and the other one idly twirling one of her clubs. I am about to ask if she would like to play through, but that's not the vibe I'm getting.

Smiling brightly, I reply, "He just can't help himself."

Mrs. Waterford narrows her eyes, evidently unsure if I understand what she's implying. Oh, I get it. I get it every time we dare to visit the country club. A thirty-year age gap is still not acceptable to some people here. Most have simply gotten over it.

But not her and some of her friends. All the more reason for me to avoid the locker room. No need for judg- mental confrontations.

Feeling the need to overtly jab me about my husband's age, she follows up with, "I'm sure the sooner he bends over backward right into a heart attack, all the better for you, right my dear?"

I could set her straight. I could try to reassure her that I'm in this marriage for love. I could tell her that we argued over the art school program I would attend. I'd chosen a small community college program. But he insisted on paying for art school in Europe, where we took an extended honeymoon for the duration of my parents' legal shitstorm. I could tell her I wouldn't care if I never saw a dime of Warrick's money if and when something terrible happens.

I could also tell her to fuck off.

But what would be the point?

If people can't see that I'm not a child and capable of making adult decisions, I don't need them in my life.

Mrs. Waterford was never in my life to begin with.

Giving her a pat on the shoulder and a sympathetic look, I tell her, "One good way to prevent a heart attack at your age is to just have lots and lots and lots of sex. Like, every night. Really get the blood pumping. Just between us girls? Tell Mr. Waterford you want him to rail you; I swear you'll see those good cholesterol numbers come back up."

Mrs. Waterford rears back in disgust, clucks her tongue, and walks away.

I watch her go, and Warrick jogs up. "Fixed it for you, baby," he says, giving me a quick kiss on the temple. "What did Elaine Waterford want?"

"To blow you, I think."

He snorts, but then I swear I can sense something shift. "Too bad because I'm all yours."

Warrick turns me toward him and rests his hands on my hips. His mouth descends against mine in a sweaty, salty kiss that reminds me of our romp on the beach last year.

I hum sweetly into his mouth, enjoying his taste and his hot body pressed against mine.

"I hope you know I need some lunch first before you take me home and ravage me. I'm hungrier than usual today."

As Candace zips over to us in her green golf cart, he whispers something filthy in my ear about a giant wiener I could eat if I'm hungry.

He can still make me blush. Good thing I'm already beet red from the heat and humidity.

"Hey, cuties! My shift is about to end. Can I bring you anything from the bar?"

Warrick taps a finger against his beard. "I'll have a

refreshing Pimm's Cup, and my child bride would like a Shirley Temple."

Candace snorts. I jab Warrick in the ribs. Even at 23, he loves these jokes. He enjoys making the already-uncomfortable people even more so. He's terrible that way—the only impoliteness I can find in him in the year we've been together.

We had a brief civil ceremony on the beach where we first kissed. We had only a handful of his family show up, a couple of people from the country club, and Candace.

She's turned out to be my best friend, and I'm a little sad that we never connected on a deep level earlier. And then, I remind myself that it wasn't up to me.

"Thanks, Candace. I'll wait until lunch. Can you join us?" I ask her.

She winks. "I would, but I have a date."

I'm about to ask with whom, but then I see it. In the distance, I see Mr. Rockwell, the movie producer, waiting impatiently on the back deck of the club, staring in our direction.

I jump up and down. "You have a date with him?!"

She nods and leans in close to whisper conspiratorially. "He asked me to be his sugar baby."

I scream. "You're not going to let him, are you?"

Behind me, Warrick growls. "You want me to chat with him and let him know that that's no way to show respect to a lady and that it's time to grow up and just marry you?"

Candace shrugs and looks up at the sky in faux innocence. "Maybe I'll let him pay off my student loans and my mom's medical bills and then make him fall in love with me instead."

Looking past her, I smile. "I don't think that will take long."

We share a friendly hug, and she bounces away to fill Warrick's drink order. I watch as Rockwell stares at Candace's hip swing as she passes by.

Watching their interaction gets both me and Warrick worked up at lunchtime. We grab our food to go and buzz home as quickly as possible.

"Outdoor shower. Now."

I love it when he takes charge of me because it always leads to something fun.

Since the wedding, Warrick installed a pool with a huge deck, a tall, private hedge, a hot tub, and an outdoor shower. We prefer this one for the concrete floors that offer more friction than a regular tub—A safety measure when things turn frisky. Especially on days like this, when we're both hot and sweaty, and he can't wait to put his face between my legs.

The growling and insistent lapping soon has me catching my breath and my thighs trembling.

"Oh, Warrick, oh my god."

We haven't even turned the water on, and I'm drenching his face, coating his beard in my essence and salt and sweat.

Riding his face like this is beyond delicious.

Thank god no one can hear us on this corner lot, especially now that my parents have moved away.

After their house was seized, Warrick paid off the back taxes and made sure all parishioners had their money and donations returned to them. Then, he bought the house. He's thinking of having it torn down and letting me build a community garden.

Now, Warrick is building me up into a crazed frenzy of need with his lashing tongue around my clit, while his fingers fill my wanton cunt. He propels me to a brain-melting orgasm. I thrust my fingers into Warrick's hair and cram my pussy into his face while he murmurs appreciative sounds. His deep, masculine noises vibrate through my body, drawing out spasm after spasm of pleasure.

Exhausted from a morning of golf under the hot sun, followed by rousing oral sex, my knees officially give out.

Warrick scoops me up, cradling me in his arms while he stands and waits for the water to reach the right temperature.

When he lovingly washes me off, we talk about plans for the garden.

"I think I'd like to add a playground. A sandbox, a swing set. Stuff like that," I tell Warrick while he soaps up my tits. My tits are the least dirty thing on my body, but he loves to make sure they are extra clean. Or so you'd think with the amount of attention he pays to them in the shower.

"Hm," he says. "I don't really feel like looking out our bedroom window onto a bunch of other people's kids screeching and crying."

I snort. Sometimes he can be such a surly hermit.

Tracing one finger down his sternum, I ask, "What if it's our kids?"

Warrick lifts one shoulder. "Sure. I mean. We'll have to build a spot for them to play one day."

"How about now?" I hook one arm around his shoulder. He smiles. "Now? I don't have the tools."

I reply, "You have only one tool I care about, and it already did the most important job."

"Baby, you're so cryptic sometimes."

He's just not catching on. Maybe I'm being too subtle.

"Warrick. Your tool put a baby in me. So get busy building a playset," I say, laughing.

This moment where I watch the wheels turn in his

head, and then the lightbulb go on is one of the sweetest moments of my life.

"You're...you're pregnant?" He bites his bottom lip to stop it from trembling.

"Are you surprised? It's not like we ever use protection."

Warrick lets out a noise that's part laugh, part shock, part roar. "We're having a baby?"

I nod, a knot forming in my throat. He looks so lost between choosing an emotion that, for half a second, I wonder if he's happy.

"I'm sorry, I didn't tell you I was taking a test. I mean, I guess we could have talked about birth control...."

Without another word, Warrick has me wrapped up in an overwhelming embrace. My legs have nowhere else to go but around his waist. He kisses me hard, his body shaking against mine. I'm crying and laughing along with him.

"A playground, a garden, a kiddie pool, a nursery, whatever you need, it's yours."

"I know. I know," I say, pressing a kiss to his nose—his beautiful nose that I first noticed about him in profile on the first day we met.

"I love you so much, and our little nugget," he says.

"I know. We love you too."

"What...what are we gonna name it?" he asks.

I already know the answer. "If it's a boy? David. If it's a girl, I'd like to name her Kahlo."

He pauses and bites his lip again. "Oh fuck, I don't care. Whatever you want. You're giving me a baby; we can call it Grogu for all I care."

Sometimes, it's frightening how much power I have over this man. I only have to say the word, and he's right behind me, backing me up no matter what. In turn, I let him love me, and I let him see how much I love myself.

I know everyone says it's important to love myself before I learn how to love a man, but things don't always work out that way in our world.

And speaking from personal experience, learning how to do both simultaneously has given me my wings. I hope I never come back down to earth.

THE END

Thank you for reading Her Devil Next Door! If you enjoyed it, don't miss out on the final story in the May December romance series, In Favor of Forever by Haven Rose.

Check the next page to make sure you're all caught up with the rest of the silver foxes...

READ ALL THE MAY DECEMBER ROMANCES!

Do you like age gap romances?

Your favorite steamy romance authors have gathered their dirty minds to bring you a selection of hot older men who won't let a little thing like age stand in the way of claiming their feisty younger women.

Age is nothing but a number, and these sexy alpha heroes know true love when they see it.

They're older, wiser, and know how to care for ALL of their woman's needs.

Come along for the ride and find out why there is no substitute for EXPERIENCE.

Check out the entire series here.

We'll Always Have Paris by Matilda Martel

The Widower Takes a Wife by Bree Weeks

The Deal with Love by Karla Doyle

Bedside Manner by Violet Rae

Dirty Secret by M.K Moore

Comedy of Wrongs by Layne Daniels

Changing Lanes by Andie Fenichel

His Wild Rebel by Ember Davis

Finding Love in Italy by Ja'Nese Dixon

Angel by Moonlight by Tamrin Banks

Forbidden Office Daddy by Carmen Falcone

Snowed in with Silver by Katharine O'Neill

Owned by the Silver Fox by Imani Jay

Forbidden Muse by Alana Winters

Missed Connections by Willow Sanders

Mountain Man's Obsession by Pippa Lux

Her Devil Next Door by Abby Knox

In Favor of Forever by Haven Rose

MORE BY ABBY KNOX

Need more short novellas?

The Naughty Yachties series

Shipped (marriage of convenience/insta love)

Secret Baby on Board (one night stand)

Wrecked (enemies to lovers)

Decked (grumpy/sunshine; chaperone)

Roped (boss/employee, age gap)

The Roadside Attractions series

Roadside Attraction (insta love)

Claiming Fate (rivals to lovers)

Falling into Fate (former best friends/second chance)

Fate's Dark Shadows (age gap)

Rode Hard (insta-love/Thanksgiving)

Crash into Me (forced proximity)

Snowed Under (later in life/forced proximity/one night stand)

The Homemade Heat series

Judge Me (age gap)

Cake Walk (age gap/dad's best friend)

Hand-Tossed (boss/employee)

*Chef's Kiss (boss/employee; boss steals the bride —
no cheating!)*

Bite Me (age gap)

*And plenty more on my website:
authorabbyknox.com*

ABOUT THE AUTHOR

Abby Knox writes feel-good, high-heat romance that she herself would want to read. Readers have described her stories as quirky, sexy, adorable, and hilarious. All of that adds up to Abby's overall goal in life: to be kind and to have fun!

Abby's favorite tropes include: Forced proximity, opposites attract, grumpy/sunshine, age gap, boss/employee, fated mates/insta-love, and more. Abby is heavily influenced by Buffy the Vampire Slayer, Gilmore Girls, and LOST. But don't worry, she won't ever make you suffer like Luke & Lorelai.

If any or all of that connects with you, then you came to the right place.

Say hello at authorabbyknox@gmail.com

Find all important links, and sign up for my newsletter, at authorabbyknox.com